BLAKE'S THERAPY

BLAKE'S THERAPY

A NOVEL BY

ARIEL DORFMAN

SEVEN STORIES PRESS

New York | London | Toronto | Sydney

Seven Stories Press
140 Watts Street
New York, NY 10013
http://www.sevenstories.com

In Canada:
Hushion House, 36 Northline Road, Toronto, Ontario M4B 3E2

Library of Congress Cataloging-in-Publication Data
Dorfman, Ariel.
    Blake's therapy / Ariel Dorfman.-Seven Stories Press 1st ed.
      p. cm.
    ISBN 1-58322-070-4 (hbk.)
      I. Title
PR9309.9.D67 B5818 2001b
813'.54-dc21

                                          00-051016

College professors may order examination copies of Seven Stories Press titles for a free six-month trial period. To order, visit www.sevenstories.com/textbook, or fax on school letterhead to (212) 226-1411.

Book design by Cindy LaBreacht.

Part title epigraphs from The Divine Comedy by Dante Alighieri, translated by John Ciardi. © 1954, 1957, 1959, 1960, 1961, 1965, 1967, 1970 by the Ciardi Family Publishing Trust. Used by permission of W.W. Norton & Company, Inc.

Printed in the U.S.A.

9 8 7 6 5 4 3 2 1

THANK YOU, RODRIGO.

"We have to distinguish between playing
by the rules and making the rules."

—GEORGE SOROS
The New York Times

"Segismundo: Is it time to wake up?
Clotaldo: Yes. The time has come to wake up."

—PEDRO CALDERÓN DE LA BARCA
Life Is a Dream

FIRST PART

"I am a shade," my Guide and Master said,
"who leads this living man from pit to pit
to show him Hell as I have been commanded."

—DANTE, INFERNO, CANTO XXIX, 94-96

ONE

I want you to take a good look at him. I
want you to take a good lazy look at
Graham Blake. True, you'll get tired of
looking at him during this coming
month of therapy. Some of you
may get tired of having him look
at you. But now's the chance,
now that there's no pressure and
you haven't met our new patient yet,
go ahead, spend some time with him at
your leisure, plunge into him. Before he
walks through that door and turns his consid-
erable charms on you and you begin to entertain
doubts as to whether he really requires this painful
treatment I have prescribed for him.

You can see the answer by yourselves: Blake is a sick
man, a man broken, delirious, needing our help more than he
can divine. Just watch him pack his bags for this trip to our

Clinic. Can you recognize the symptoms? The way the fingers shake—
only the index finger firm—as he smooths the shirts, discards the blue-
and-white striped tie his lover's given him for Christmas, stares at that
tie for several seconds as if it were about to snake up and sting him.
Remark how he retrieves it with a hand that cannot stop trembling,
folds it uncertainly, can't fit it into the bag so it won't crumple. Look at
how he waves away the valet—that's Hector, who's trying to be of assistance—angrily shoos him out the door, sinks onto the bed, our Graham
takes his head in his hands as if it were about to roll off a cliff, those
hands rubbing downward to the eyes, massaging eyes that have not
slept in so many days that he's lost count. But we haven't. Lost count,
I mean. We know it's been ninety-five days that he hasn't managed
more than one or two hours a night, some nights nothing at all. Staying up till dawn, even knockout pills only working for a few minutes and
then he's up again, desperate drunken eyes wide open, sitting rigid for
hours in the dark just like he's sitting now, those slender pianist fingers
of his scraping and stroking his temples, the headache that will not go
away. Ninety-five days exactly since that headache kicked in, the everlasting midnights, his crisis, his rage at himself and everything. His
doubts, his endless self-doubts.

Now look at how our future patient calls Hector in, apologizes for
having lost his temper, lets the valet carefully take care of the clothes,
the tie, how Graham Blake twitches his head ironically when Hector
asks him if he'll be needing condoms. Is that a yes? Is that a no? Even
Blake is not clear what he himself answered. What is clear is how he
smiles now at his valet. See that smile? It changes his whole face, it's
easy to understand why Hector likes his boss, would do anything to
make him happy, why we have to be wary of falling under Blake's influence while he's here.

Conclusions, just from this snap of a scene?

Graham Blake is a man used to giving orders. Graham Blake does
not like mistreating others, especially subordinates. Graham Blake has
more charm than is good for him, he covers up his mistakes with that

smile, since he's been a child he's smiled his way out of every mistake he's ever made. Graham Blake may be used, therefore, to getting what he wants, but isn't willing to pay the price. He cares, perhaps excessively, about how the world perceives him, what others say about him.

So this is going to take some time. The treatment. Longer than he expects, longer than I let on when I apprised him at the end of our inaugural session of the extreme measures necessary to remedy his quasi-terminal anguish, relieve him of the condition that medical journals in the future may well call Tolgate's syndrome.

So. Who is this man?

Graham Blake, forty-three years old. Mother died when he was six. Father died when he was eighteen. Two children, one boy, one girl. Divorced. Happily divorced. Meaning it was a good divorce. No cheating on his wife, no beating up on each other, no lawsuits. No bickering in front of the kids, Thomas and Georgina, cute little things, later you can take a look at some outtakes from home movies, courtesy of Graham Blake, model parent. A perfect divorce, perfect and quick like most things in Graham Blake's quick life. Not that he had much choice: He was in partnership, still is, with his wife, Jessica Owen, bioengineer. Kept her maiden name. Yes. A woman bioengineer, specializing in gene manipulation. You must have come across her name. A genius. Candidate for a double Nobel, in Medicine and in Chemistry. And might even bag the Nobel Peace Prize to boot. Not her only attributes: Take a glance at this photo. Not a bad looker, huh? That intensity, that high forehead, those cheekbones, nice full body too, works out for two hours each morning. *Mens sana*, etc. Because she is the brains of the Company. Oh, he's smart, but not as smart as she is. Indispensable, however, our Graham. So far. So far.

He's the organizer, the partner who's able to tap into the dreams and desires of a billion potential clients, the marketing guru—been selling a benign image of himself to others since he was a youngster, been selling a similar image of his products, his Company, Solving the Energy Crisis, Solving the Food Crisis, Solving the Health Crisis. But he only really took off, flourished, left the heavy load of his past behind, when Jessica swept into his life, at a time they were both doing postgrad work at Stanford. Jessica Owen injected the scientific know-how into Clean Earth that made it a corporate leader in biodiversity, global excellence, responsibility. "We Change Mother Earth Without Hurting Her." Whatever that means, it works. Success, esteemed colleagues and staff, is what works. For Graham Blake, for us.

And for Jessica Owen, she's the one, after all, who made Graham Blake, turned him into who he is. She's been like a mother to him, the mother he lost as a child. When Graham Blake met her, he was the owner of one dump of a factory that manufactured traditional cosmetic and herbal products here in Philadelphia. Yes, right here, ladies and gentlemen, in this very city where we await him, where he'll be heading as soon as Hector finishes packing, as soon as he's said good-bye to Natasha. There she is, Natasha, Blake's lover, on the screen, he's not happy about leaving her for a month, he's not happy about being separated from those flashing eyes, those breasts, even if he hasn't fondled them lately, can barely manage to bring himself to touch her skin, caress her rump. You can be sure he did not readily agree to our demand that he come alone to Philadelphia, the city where his father's old factory is still chugging along, not two miles south of here, in a less affluent neighborhood, of course, than ours. Jessica Owen used the slim profits from the soap, the make-up creams, the herb concoctions of that factory to build the Blake empire. Now they produce, in twenty-two locations in these United States, an array of vitamins, herbal wonders, stimulants, floral essences, Magical Foods, Enchanted Nutrients, Oils for the Soul, Youth Pills, the Over-and-Over-Again Supplements that have enhanced our sexuality, the Miracle Muscle Potions for joggers with weak knees. And the Time-Stretchers, oh yes, those energy pills that make you work faster all the while slowing down with herbs your perception of normal time? Our Graham invented the names, packaged the goods, identified the needs, but it is his wife—former wife—who made it all possible, first through her own lab work and later by approaching the academic researchers at anthropology departments at the major universities and soon after that their Botany and Forestry and Environmental Studies programs. She enlisted professors and graduate students to become the gatherers and collectors of seeds and plants, purveyors of flowers and leaves, from the Amazon, Borneo, Zambia. Then Blake came up with the winning formula, pasted it on every billboard: "The Earth Knows the Answer." I'm telling you, be careful of Blake, beware of his imagination. Just look at the toys that he invented, the family of plastic rainforest monkeys free with every purchase, the rainbow of birds on cereal covers for the children and the dancing iguanas on the vitamin supplements for sick women and the movie tie-ins and the cds with live animal sounds combined with native chanting and rock stars chiming in and the eco-computers-into-schools project and the amusement parks. And then Graham convinced his board of directors to branch out into spas and eco-tourism and an array of Rainbow Hotels.

THE COMPANY THAT SAVED THE RAINFOREST—remember that cover on *Time* magazine? Graham Blake is interviewed in that number. The editor explains that there is no photo of the CEO because Blake did not allow any to be snapped—further proof, if any were needed, of his modesty. Or was it something else, hiding inside that man who doesn't flaunt his image? Not that he thinks so. "I do not deserve," he declared with surprising frankness, "any special recognition. It's a matter of survival. What's good for the earth, is good for the Company. If there aren't trees, roots, shrubs, there can be no extraction. No extraction and this Company goes bankrupt. It's that simple."

So how did things go wrong? Exactly what happened ninety-five days ago, when his crisis began? The details matter only marginally. You've seen the problem enough in the last years. Prosperity leads to overexpansion and cutthroat competition from rival firms with lower costs and less personnel benefits and aggressive outsourcing to India and Brazil. Then a sharp drop in demand from Asia, bankruptcies in Latin America, diminished returns from European outlets, and suddenly no liquidity to pay for loans. So Blake's Company was in a weakened position when none other than Hank Granger mounted a hostile takeover. You may recall that Mr. Granger has been for several years to acquire a Company that would offer him a chance to clean up his tarnished corporate image. Clean Earth fit the bill. Let me say no more. As we have all had the chance in the past to get acquainted with Mr. Granger's methods...

Graham Blake, in order to keep Clean Earth out of Mr. Granger's eager hands, was forced to downsize, rid himself of many trusted employees. Too late. Because Blake had held up this overdue internal restructuring for far too long, he could not avoid his board's peremptory demand to close down one of his two Philadelphia operations and relocate it to Mexico. His decision, when it came exactly ninety-five days ago, made no economic sense: He uprooted the more recent, high-tech plant, the profitable one, and kept open the original cosmetics and herb factory, with its obsolete technology, its astronomical deficit, its safety accidents.

Accused of having too soft a heart by the board, Blake argued that this was a great public relations ploy: It would show Clean Earth as a Company that stood by its gut loyalties, did not abandon its origins or the solidarity ethics of the rainforest communities that were the ultimate source of its riches, at the very moment when the Company was, in fact, doing the opposite, moving abroad in search of more profits, succumbing to the bottom-line rationale it had sworn never to embrace.

What he did not say, what Jessica Owen harshly berated him for later in no uncertain terms—you can watch the exchange on tape at your convenience—was that he was deluding himself. He was saving that old factory for purely sentimental reasons: It was the one where his past lay, where he got started before he met her. He wanted, she said, to hold on to one thing that she had not touched, upgraded, changed. And this gem: "You're just postponing what you always knew you'd have to do. Destroy your past. The hard choice. Growing up, Graham. Growing up is the really hard choice."

The board of directors also questioned his judgment, although Blake finally charmed them into agreement. "We have been worrying about hurting the earth," one faithful member who'd reluctantly sided with Blake is reported to have said on his way out of the meeting. "Maybe it's time to worry more about hurting our stockholders."

One would think that Graham Blake's principled stand ("I will not sit by and condone the ravaging of the lives of workers and employees here in our country, the erosion of Company loyalty, the damage to Clean Earth's image, in order to pursue illusory profits beyond the borders of America"—look at his clenched telegenic jaw, the gloss in his eyes, that dangerous smile of his when he confronts Jessica afterward in his office), one might have predicted that such a stance would calm his conscience, leave it like the surface of a lake on a windless day, all misgivings about his morality put to rest. No such thing. That very night brings his first bout of insomnia and the next day, with his head exploding, he makes a series of hasty business transactions that Jessica Owen is able to block before their potentially calamitous implementation.

An example? Certainly.

Do you remember the first time any of you stepped into your bathroom at a hotel and saw a sign suggesting you make the right ecological choice and reuse your towels rather than having them replaced? Yes. You know: Be a good world citizen while you dry yourself. Graham Blake was the mastermind behind that idea, now adopted everywhere: a way of saving, true, an enormous amount of energy and electricity. But what he—and the managers of hotels—never informed the guests was how that also meant reducing the cost of washing and resupplying the towels. Well, that first day of crisis Blake wanted to call a press conference—Blake, who hated publicity, who didn't want his picture anywhere, who never shows himself—Blake wanted to announce a new Transparency Campaign: from now on the Rainbow Hotels were going to pass on to the guests themselves the profits made by recycling the towels. Just one example of Blake's anguish. "Transparency Campaign?"

Jessica thundered. "Call it by its name, a Stupidity Campaign, that's what it is. A Corporate Suicide Campaign." And she nixed it.

And that's how it went for the next three months, the same pattern of Blake behaving erratically, unpredictably, and Jessica blocking each irresponsible decision. But it wasn't only his business acumen that began to suffer and go sour, but his personal life, his sex life in particular. Here, take a look at this video: no erection despite the voluptuous promptings of Natasha, again his head in his hands as he sits on the bed, this time naked and limp, trapped in some turmoil that he can barely manage to convey.

But convey it he finally does. Watch. Let me reiterate his words carefully so we don't miss the nuances. "Do you think I'm a good man?" Note the little-boy plaintiveness with which he asks this of Natasha a few nights later after another of their unsatisfactory sexual clinches has ended in defeat.

And Natasha's crucial answer: "The best," she says, and means it. The best man in the world. The most generous. High drama.

"No, really," Graham Blake asks again. "Good not because it looks good. Good because it comes from inside, deep inside."

And she reassures him. She dutifully points out how Clean Earth pioneers ways of saving the environment in faraway lands, is working on eliminating another famine in Ethiopia, and even so, he never takes any credit. She strokes his ego and tries to stroke his body. To no avail. An indication of—? That's right: that he's obsessed not with what he did but with what he may yet do. Haunted by an ethical question that lies not in the past but ahead, in the future.

Watch this series of sequential photos, so similar to those you've seen of our other patients, the same Immorality Syndrome that I hope will someday bear my name in the annals of medicine. Watch how Graham Blake begins to age—those are real gray hairs he is trying to dye brown. Watch him hop, like our other desperate clients, from one doctor to another, from psychologist to psychiatrist to accupuncturist to homeopathic herbal expert, a constellation of quacks who do not have the formula because only we have it at this Institute. Watch the obvious, the inevitable: How things deteriorate at the office, how he strikes Thomas, his eldest child, and then enshrouds him with kisses. Watch how in the course of one morning he fires and then subsequently rehires his secretary, Miss Jenkins, buys her flowers, raises her salary, throws the coffee she brings him across the room because it has a tad too much cream—need I go on? It's the same sorry story of so many chief executives who flounder through identical trials and tribulations before they are steered to us.

Graham Blake, in fact, is lucky. On average, it takes most patients ten to twelve months to detect our existence from the moment of their initial crisis. Of course, we'd been monitoring Blake's case for a while, since signs first surfaced and information was passed on that he would soon be coming our way. Blake took a shortcut to us courtesy of Sam Halneck, whom I am sure you all remember. Mr. Halneck, who sailed through our therapy clinic with flying colors and looks twenty years younger now than when he entered for his treatment, having entirely overcome any guilt feelings an overanxious mother and a sneering step-father instilled in him at an early age, happens to be Graham Blake's best friend—and he and his wife, Miriam, along with Natasha, of course, and not to forget Jessica Owen with her ultimatum—they all convinced Blake that he should visit me, that Dr. Carl Tolgate would cure him of all this nonsense.

Which brings us to one last item. Money.

Notice now how Blake, before leaving the penthouse, peels off several hundred-dollar bills, slips them into Hector's pocket unobtrusively, does not want to embarrass his valet. Pays him back for that outburst we witnessed just a short while ago. So it would seem that our subject does not give a damn about money, couldn't care less. If you ask him for ten, he'll give you twenty. Let me click on another scene now, while Graham Blake goes down in the elevator, Hector, of course, carrying his bags. Look at this: It's when I explained our fees to him. You deposit three million dollars with us in escrow. Except for ten percent, which goes to cover expenses, no questions asked, we won't touch the rest of the sum until the end of your month and only if you are totally satisfied. We are as sure, Mr. Blake, of our products as you are of yours. You sell a Clean Earth. We sell a Clean Conscience.

You see. You see how he does not allow the slightest doubt or demurral to creep into his wrist, his elbow, the tips of his fingers, as he signs that check for three million dollars. Of course, he knew I was looking at him, he knew my eye was upon him, he might even have suspected that a camera was rolling in my consulting room. Though he has no idea that he is being filmed right now as he leaves his home to pick up his flight from Houston and fly here, no idea that last night, for instance, he was being taped at dinner. Here, let me fastforward to the moment when Sam Halneck is ordering the best wine on the menu. A Château Lafitte, is it? Costs around $350. Graham is paying. Graham is smiling. You see that smile? Beware of that smile. But now he turns sharply and the camera captures his eyes narrowing, now that his face is away from Sam and Sam's wife, Miriam, and Natasha, now that they can't observe him, look at how Graham's eyes narrow and darken. It's not stinginess. He can afford hundreds of bottles like that one. He could buy the whole restaurant, he might even own it already. The darkness ruffling his eyes: If I can indulge in a metaphor, it's as if a bird flies into a windowpane and falls to the ground inside those eyes. A flower fading inside the mother of his eyes. That momentary darkness, that quickly dispelled darkness, is a sign that he is worried that others will take advantage of his goodwill toward all men. Though there may be something more unsettling, deeper than my immediate diagnosis indicates. The snap of his fingers as he pays the bill, that impatience and self-assurance. Not that he expects attention right away. He expects it before he snaps his fingers. He expects others to guess what he wants before he even knows it himself. Instant satisfaction. Satisfaction before he can formulate the desire.

Now. Rewind to that moment just now when he deposited those bills in Hector's pocket. Look at his hands: There is a slight quivering as the bills go into the pocket, our camera picks up that trembling touch that Graham Blake himself is unaware of. A tremor that tells us that we cannot be sure how Graham Blake would react if he were not to possess that money, if he were to face a situation where he might forfeit the possibility of paying for a vintage wine from thirty years ago, or of leaving several hundred dollars as a tip, or be unable to buy two horses for his kids as going-away presents, do without the original Francis Bacon painting that hangs over the bed he fruitlessly shares with Natasha. If he did not have the chance to fill the void around him and inside him by easily spreading his charitable wings, doing good, solving the food crisis, answering the energy crisis, brilliantly intervening in the towel crisis, what would happen if he could not think the world of himself as he is saving the world and the Amazon Indians. Just something for you all to chew on.

Any doubts? Dilemmas? Moral reservations?

Now is the time to bring them up. Now that he's only an image on this screen. Once he's materialized, once he steps across that threshold in the flesh and begins to hate where he is and announces that what we are proposing is immoral and that he's leaving immediately, once he decides a few hours later, as all our patients do, to stay, once he is sucked into the vortex of his therapy and sees it through to its inevitable and illuminating end—then there will be no time to repent or pull out, then I don't expect any of you to protest to me that you can't stand another minute of this. Our slogan—read it carefully, memorize it: "If the Patient Can Stand It, So Can the Therapists." The whole gang of you. Is that clear?

Just remember. This is all being done—every last horrible thing—for his own good.

We're going to save Graham Blake in spite of himself.

TWO

Can you hear me, Roxanna, my Roxanna,
not mine, not mine? I think you can.
Even if you never acknowledge my eyes
on your flowing body, not with so
much as a waver over there, on the
other side of the glass, never
return this gaze that follows
you from room to room, from
hidden camera to hidden microphone. I think you know somebody
like Graham Blake is here, watching you.
Watching how you undress by yourself in
the evening, without your lover to cover that
foot of yours with a sheet, always slipping, that
foot of yours, out from under. Without your lover
because I have him in jail, it's me, I think you know there
is someone like me who has your Johnny in prison on
trumped-up charges. You must have wondered at some point
during this last perverse month of my therapy if there wasn't a

man sitting here on the blind other side of the wall of your apartment, enjoying how you brush the black cascade of your hair in front of the mirror while my eyes stare into your unsuspecting eyes not five inches away. Enjoying how you linger on the toilet and press the two flanks of your little ass together. I know your secret. Not even Johnny knows or knew, I'm sure he never found out that this is the way you defecate, make it emerge soundlessly so the rest of the family can't tell, no matter how much they keep snooping, that bastard of your father would love to get his hands on that rump, those thighs, or simply get near to you by eavesdropping on the sound, let it drop into his ears. But you thwart him, you thwart everybody but me, it comes out so low and slow that I'm the only one who can hear it. Maybe it's a performance for me. Me. This man you supposedly don't guess even exists, has been here for the last four weeks, watching. Not only watching. Forging your existence. Weren't those Dr. Tolgate's words? My therapy: Roxanna. That's how Dr. Tolgate put it, said you were my little therapy. "There she is, Graham," he said, "the woman who will cure you of your mental sickness. Do with her, with all of them, what you will."

"Do? What do you mean?"

Whatever I wanted. Anything. Everything. To you, to your lousy father, to your hoop-crazy kid brother, your distraught mom, your— everybody that belongs to you. Even kill them, you, anything.

"You mean I can kill her?"

"You can kill her," Tolgate answered.

I was indignant, began to say it was immoral, it—

"Only if you kill her," Tolgate interrupted me, his eyes glinting behind his glasses as if they were also behind some sort of window. "If you don't hurt her at all, in spite of having her at your fingertips, then you're confirming how truly ethical you are. Look, Graham—you don't mind if I call you—"

"Call me Blake." Cold, trenchant, angry.

"Then Blake. If you've never had the chance to really kill someone, Blake, you can never find out if you're a murderer, can you?"

I was furious, Roxanna. They could keep their ten percent for operating expenses, that doctor could shove my three-hundred-thousand-dollar guarantee up his ass. Well, didn't quite say it that way. I was more elevated, more dignified. I suspected they were taping me, didn't want anything embarassing on tape. Misgivings I've had since I was a child, since the day when my father opened the Christmas gift from Mom, her last gift to him before she…, he opened it and there was an 8 mm Kodak film camera, the kind with which families used to record their everyday lives, and he was so happy, until I refused to be filmed. It was irrational, that fear. Which grew through the day and continued on into the night, when I was so scared that I couldn't sleep and crept down the stairs to the living room and I stole the family picture album and there, among the toys and wrappings and the smell of dead and dying pine, I started to rub out my face in each and every one of the photos where I appeared. At times that makes me sad, you know, because I don't have even one photo with my mother, not even one. Nobody has a picture of me, nobody at all. I could walk into your living room right now and you'd have no idea who I was, that I'm the man who owns your factory.

That was the first hook, the first bait, that Tolgate used. That you were all involved, or had been, in one way or another, with my Company. All the members of that family, even the most important one, the woman who hasn't arrived on the scene yet, Tolgate said. Strange that you weren't there in that room over there, Roxanna, when he began to explain the therapy.

I woke up. They had drugged me on the way from the airport, insisted it was imperative that I not see where I was being taken. When I clambered out of my deepest sleep in months, there he was, Dr. Carl Tolgate, standing in the middle of the control room, all the screens lighting up behind him like enormous insect eyes in the wall, all the knobs twisting like bugs on fire. I must have looked startled with the hell-like imagery: He gave me time to recompose myself, take a shower, change into something more informal. Then he introduced me to

Sonia and Sandra. My keepers. Also yours. Even if you haven't an inkling, Roxanna. Or do you? Why can't I shake the conviction that you're aware of what I'm doing, Sonia and Sandra are doing at my command, to you and your family, how we've been playing with you, with that slob of your father.

Sorry to call him that. I know you adore him, Roxanna, but I really don't like, don't trust the guy.

"Will you look at that," Tolgate said to me a few nights ago when you kissed your father good night and his fingers loitered on your breast and then descended to tickle your midriff. "He's abused her, Blake, it's a textbook case. And yet, she loves the guy, so she's forgiven him or she's forgotten or maybe she's incapable of ill will toward anybody. I mean, who knows what goes on in that brain of hers."

I looked as he suggested and admired how you extricated yourself from your father's embrace, softened the grip of his fingers, covered his eyes with the bird of your hand, blew him a kiss from afar, crossed to the room you used to share with Jason, before I sent him off to—... Jason, I do like. Proof is how well your kid brother's been doing for the last month, thriving since I've been around. I followed you to that room, kept you in my sights even after you turned off the light, when I ordered Sonia—or was it Sandra?—to flood you with infrared so I could watch you breathe rhythmically in the dark, commanded a close-up of your chest slackening up and down, up and down, swooping in the air that is not the air I breathe on this side, unwilling to go to bed myself. Aware that time is running out. Yes. Running out. Ending. And that I had to relish the moment. And make amends, put things right.

Yes, for your father as well. He'll get his job back, your mom will win back the money I made that gang steal from her food stand, your lover will be out of jail. I'm even making sure you'll be able to return to Puerto Rico, set up an export business of herbs. The Latino Leaf you'll call it, or maybe Roxanna's Magical Herbs. I know marketing if I know anything, Roxanna, and I can guarantee a stunning success, just like I told Sonia. I laid the whole plan out to her. She was a bit dubious, I can tell. But who cares what she thinks? Sonia's job is to obey the boss, to be as efficient in bettering your life tomorrow as she was destroying it over the last month.

She's arranging it right now, a happy ending, Sonia is. Even as I watch you on our last night together, my Roxanna mine, we who have never been together, who never will be together. Unless I can convince Sonia to…. Unless I manage a last-minute expedition into your territory. Last chance. Tomorrow I'll be gone, I'll be back with my Natasha and you—you'll be making slow love on that bed where you now sit in a tantra position and meditate langourously. Imagining something that makes you smile. I'll never know, I guess, what makes you really smile. Hoping that it's me, hoping that you conjecture a benefactor like me coming to the rescue, ending your troubles so you can smile for a reason.

It's going to happen no matter what. Because if Sonia can't organize an immediate solution to all those problems I've created, well, then, I'll take care of things tomorrow. Nobody can stop me from hiring anybody I want in any of our enterprises. You're in my territory, Roxanna, after all, have been for years. You only have work because I decided to keep your factory open and close the other one where your mom and Ned were employed, tit for tat, they lost their jobs so you could keep yours.

I had to do it, Roxanna. I'm sure you wouldn't understand my rationale, seeing it was that decision of mine to relocate the factory to Mexico that created the turmoil in your family, the suicide of a friend of yours who worked there.

"Strange that after so many years at your service," the doctor said when he pointed them out to me for the first time, that first day, "now they're going to work for you one more time, and this time they won't know it either. Look at them, take a lazy look: the people who will help you to reach deep into the mystery of what's happening to you, help you on your road to mental health."

"Help me?"

"You're going to use them to work through whatever it is that's not letting you sleep."

"Use them?"

I had not yet got my bearings, could not quite unravel what this was all about. They were over there, all of them, except you: your dad, your mom, Jason, Ned, and that stupid fool friend of your father's who mopes and whines all day, as if the world owed him something, as if the world had done something terrible to him, that idiot Fred with his paralyzed left arm. All of them, not knowing that they were on the menu. They were my menu. Soon I'd decide which one to eat, which one to spare, what over the next month I would—

"Use them," Tolgate repeated. "Be their God. And enact upon them the scenario from heaven or from hell your heart desires, the good, the bad, the detestable, the sublime. Lift them up or grind them into the earth. Go as far as you want: the only leash, your imagination. The limit, your will. Or…"

He let his voice trail off. Or what?

I was groggy from the drugs, the first complete hours of blessed unconsciousness I had dropped into in three months. The shower had been vigorous, but somehow I felt as if I were still sleeping. He had to be joking. Roxanna, I didn't take him seriously, didn't even protest what he was proposing until you came in. By then he had been droning on for a while in that sedate, rumbling voice of his: "Let's start with the author of the most important person in this family."

"The author?" I asked.

"The father, the progenitor," said Tolgate impatiently. "The author of her days, of the woman you have yet to meet and who holds the key to your recovery. There, that's Bud. An ex-marine, met the mother, that's Silvia, they met in Puerto Rico, got her pregnant with—well, you'll see with who. It must have been quite a night of love because— well, you'll see, as I said, what came of it. Though their other two offspring are quite nicely rounded as well. That's Jason. He'd die to be able to make it big in basketball—which you can arrange, Blake, I can assure you, Sonia here can make it all happen with the snap of a finger. Not quite. I'm exaggerating. I get excited with the array of possibilities open to our patients. One of my little faults that you'll learn to forgive. It will take more than the snap of a finger. At times there's a delay, the gratification is not always instantaneous. But three million dollars—there's a reason, Blake, why our price is so steep. To make things happen in this city, we need a lot of cash. Cash. It can help the kid speed straight to the top. Or it can deliver a little accident. And then our Jason will be in a wheelchair for life. Once that's happened, of course, we can't reverse it. I mean, you have to be careful what you ask for. Remember that some things, once they've happened—no rewind button, no innocently returning things to how they were. If someone, for instance, were to trip Jason up and he fell in front of a car—we can't predict the consequences, that's what I mean. That's what your therapy is about, why it works so well: It's real."

That's when I was on the verge of opening my mouth, telling him to fuck off if he was serious and he could also fuck off if he was trying to make fun of me, that's when you made your grand entrance, almost as if you were a movie star. It was as if Tolgate had foreshadowed that I was about to insult him, as if he had planned a diversion, because you streamed into the room. As if on cue. As if to silence me. *Streamed* is the wrong word, Roxanna. I've been trying to figure it out, how you walk, what you do to your own body to make it that luminous—not the right word either. What you do is to take just a swaying fraction more time than anybody else I know, as if you were living in a slightly delayed form of motion or, better still, as if the rest of the universe were accelerated and you haven't allowed its mad rhythm to drown you. Or maybe I'm imagining this. I've only seen you, of course, in the context of your family and they're all a nervous, jittery bunch, unhappy with their fate, unhappy with what my faraway arrangement three months ago to shut down that plant did to their life. But not you. You take everything in your stride. Your gentle, drawling stride.

"There's your little therapy now," Tolgate said. "There she is, Graham. Think of it: she works as a nurse in your factory. And now she's going to nurse you back to reality."

Reality. The real hook, the real bait, the real fish, the real water. You. The reason Tolgate chose this family of all possible families for me to adopt, to use, abuse, elevate, bring down, help cure my insomnia, my headaches gone, my aggressiveness taken out on you and yours, squeezed out of me minute by minute just as the doctor promised. As if you were a miracle drug.

"You'll get better," he had announced when he took me on a tour of what would be my home for the next month. "As long as you follow the rules, that is. You've got to stay inside this apartment for the next month, Blake. Isolated. No going out, no visitors, no phone calls to anybody, particularly no one from your former life. No passionate phone sex with Natasha back home. No chatting with your kids so you can bathe in their innocence. No consulting with Jessica on how the latest ad campaign is going, the newest breakthrough to help the peasants of Thailand grow better organic rice. And absolutely, positively, most definitely, no crossing over to the other side. No fraternization. You need anything, here's Sonia. Here's Sandra."

I looked them over again, as if I was only seeing now how much they looked like guards in a Nazi concentration camp, though Sonia… she was attractive in spite of the close-cropped hair, the flinty eyes, breasts a bit larger than I like them, how was I to guess that my hands would explore the shape of those breasts instead of yours, Roxanna, that my eyes would do one thing with your body, and the other thing, my hands and the length of my body would do the real thing with her, with Sonia. Doing it because of you. Because I calculated that I would need her on our side someday. Always be ready for an emergency, my dad would tell me. Don't wait for the emergency to come to you. Be prepared for it. We're only an inch from the abyss.

My dad and his famous abyss. I used to think it was some sort of monster when I was a kid, something that hissed and would swallow me up. Had taken my mother and might take me. Only later did I comprehend—as I built my Company, divorced Jessica, fought off Hank Granger's takeover, fought to keep my father's Company—what Dad really meant. When you're only one step from the abyss, boy, you'd better have a rope dangling from some nearby tree, you'd better have a life-jacket, boy. Sonia was my rope, my therapy lifejacket—and not a bad fuck at that. Also a good cook. Not as savory as Sandra. Not as quick to clean up. "They'll do your laundry, make your bed, bring you whatever you need from the outside world, carry out your orders—or rather"—and here Tolgate nodded in the direction of the four hefty hulks who were patrolling the door—"they will, Ivan and Company."

Ivan. Has to be a pseudonym, something Tolgate coined for him. A Russian name for the head honcho to terrorize me with his apparent foreignness, as if Ivan were a commissar, someone who could not be moved or bribed or even spoken to, apparently deaf. Deaf and deadly. His arms crossed in front of him like a gangster in a B-movie.

"So that's clear, then," Tolgate added. "No trespassing. You contact one member of this family the clinic has preselected for you and the experiment is over, finished. You forfeit the money and, what's worse, you forfeit the treatment. Back to insomnia for the rest of your existence. The doctoring cannot work unless you are completely subservient in this one sphere. The only rule you have to obey. Everything else, everybody else—at your service, to do your will. Obeying you, your slightest, craziest, most vicious, most delicious whim. Even God, after all, has to live according to certain rules, recognize certain limits. Like the speed of light. Knowing the one thing He can't do gives a special kick to all the things He can do. Right?"

I was hardly listening to him, I can't even remember if he said this to me before you came in or if it was afterward. Wait. It must have been afterward. If I didn't pay attention, it was because I was absorbed by your movements, it must have been because of that. As if you were lit by some special soft aura. Where did it come from? How could you glow with such joy, dance your way at your leisure through that dreadful living room packed with dreadful relatives? And then suddenly stop.

Stop in front of me, as if you were looking straight into the clandestine camera that slips and slides your image into my brain. You stopped and brought your hands together, fingers touching lightly in front of you in convocation of—what? Your eyes closing oh so indolently as if you were remembering something, somebody—what? What?

"She's praying," Tolgate said to me. He was behind me like a shadow. He seemed to fathom my thoughts. Maybe he's considered me so thoroughly while preparing this rehabilitation that he... If you had seen how his lips twisted into a slight grin, the barest of expressions, but it was there, it was there when I examined Sonia, transfixed my gaze for a second too long on the hidden cleavage of her overflowing breasts— he knew that I would soon be losing myself in those breasts because I could not cradle yours, I could not perfume my mouth with your body.

"She's religious, this Roxanna?" I asked. Because you didn't seem the sort. Puerto Rican, Catholic origin, Tolgate had murmured of the family, but that didn't quite fit you, I couldn't conjure up those knees of yours going down in front of a cross, inside a confessional booth with a salivating priest nearby, lighting a candle to the Virgin. And I was right. Tolgate made that much clear.

"Not in the traditional sense. Her mother, Silvia—she goes to mass, the works. Silvia has asked the Lord to help them now that evil times have descended on the family. When Ned gambled away their scant assets and his severance pay the afternoon he got the sack, Silvia poured what was left of her life savings into a food-cart business. So she's got reason to be anxious, to seek aid from above. Useless, of course: You're the one, Blake, who will decide how her affairs go. You can send hundreds of clients to purchase her Puerto Rican street fare and sneak her tips, tell her to keep the spare change, have her written up in the *Inquirer* so that in a month's time, before you leave, she can have miraculously stowed away enough for a down payment on a restaurant. And she's on her way to success and the family with her. Or you can screw our Silvia over. Have her raped one evening, for instance."

I ignored his insinuations. I wasn't going to collude in his shameful plot. But I didn't say so right away, truth to tell, Roxanna, because of you. I needed to know more, maybe some voice inside was suggesting that once I was free of the Infernal Doctor I could look you up, later, tomorrow, another day, soon. But I had to gather more information on you before leaving.

"If she's not religious like her mother," I said, "what in the hell is she doing now?"

Tolgate explained what you do, Roxanna, what has fascinated me during the last four weeks: the fact that you are a healer. Not just a nurse. I never knew that we were carrying out this sort of program, though Jessica once, I think, mentioned something about dabbling in alternative medicine at certain production centers, if we're marketing it to the world we might as well practice what we preach, that sort of thing. Massage, magnets, most of all herbal medicine. You gathered them when you were a child on your island. I've watched you during so many late afternoons sifting through all those leaves and teas and potions, singing in Spanish to them, to the original plants that sent you their offerings. Waiting for the next package to arrive from San Juan. The delivery that I sabotaged, ordered Sonia to hold back in the postal service to see if that made you nervous, if that made you divine the possible existence of a presence like mine, realize that some powerful creature had to be meddling with your life, held the code and password to your happiness. But I couldn't stand the way you would come home each day and interrogate your mother about the expected package of herbs from your island paradise as if you suspected her of having hidden it, I couldn't abide that discontent seeping into your shoulders, adding to the burden of Johnny's jailing and the roller-coaster ride I had ordained for the family, too many ups and downs, one too many to also deny you that magical flora you deploy to cure my employees and keep them productive, the ointments you salve them with, the massage oil from the tangled forests that saw your birth. I gave in to that sorrow inside you, told Sonia to make sure the package was delivered right away.

Right away? She arched her eyebrows. Not because she's jealous of you. She knows that you are out of bounds and that she's inside bounds, inside and under the circle of my hands. Sonia was suggesting that I might be expecting too much too soon, that I might be overdoing this. I confirmed the order. Right away. And was rewarded by your childlike awe less than an hour later as you opened your package, smelling each pulverized leaf, that foliage taking you back to when you had indeed been a girl and picked each flower, tasted the trees, breathed in what you would use in the future to dress the wounds in a Philadelphia factory that even back then belonged to me and my family. Did you start praying then? As a child, I mean?

So many things I would like to ask you, so many things I ask Tolgate. At times he answers. On other occasions he simply pleads ignorance. When did she start praying? "She's been praying forever, discovered that even if she didn't believe in a traditional, patriarchal God or go to church, she could pray for the distant patients," yes, I've seen you concentrate your mind on them, complement the tea they are sipping, the vitamins they are injecting into their immune system, help the muscles you have relaxed with those fluttering hands of yours that will never pour down my back like rain, will never clutch at my buttocks to make sure I stay firm inside you. "She discovered very early, I am sure," Tolgate surmised a few days later, "that her prayers worked, went out to the damaged, the injured, the bruised." Not healing them, I thought to myself, watching you. Opening a space inside where they could begin to heal themselves.

Not that I knew any of this in detail when I first saw you gather those hands together so that the energy flowed from one arm through to the other, the energy I could almost touch swelling along the veins or the nerves or whatever inner rivers of yours that energy needs to navigate, the energy going out to the men and women whom I pay in that factory I did not close, keeping them healthy and happy. I might not have known all of this, but I did have an intuition. Just looking at you. That was it. To see you do what was right and care for them, enough to remind me of who I was, of who I have been and tried to be all my life. Returning me to this Graham Blake who does not play with people. Who has dedicated his life to making others well and the world a better place. Who has already drawn up a will to leave eighty percent of his money to charities that deal with the homeless, minority education, dance lessons for inner-city kids, donations of video-cameras to indigenous tribes in the Amazon so that they can film themselves. The Graham Blake who broke down three months ago—and I thought to myself, maybe this is the therapy, maybe it's no more than this visit for one hour to this clinic, being able to see somebody giving and forgiving without second or third or fourth thoughts, maybe that's all I need, this flower of a girl chanting silently.

It may have been that hope—that I was cured, swiftly, painlessly, ready to go home and see my kids and Natasha—that did it, made me turn to Tolgate and say, "I'm leaving." Just like that. "I'll have nothing more to do with this depraved experiment."

"That's the normal reaction," he answered. "Everybody says the same—well, not everybody, in one case he...—but almost everybody reacts at first by rejecting any participation."

I didn't respond to that, headed for the door. Ivan blocked my path. He must measure a good head taller than me, weigh a hundred pounds more than I weigh, muscles on his arms as big as your waist, Roxanna.

"I'm afraid," Tolgate's voice called out behind me, "that you'll have to wait till tomorrow."

"Why?"

"Regulations. Security reasons. I could bullshit you with all sorts of pretexts, but here's the truth, Blake. The clinic believes that you should be given a chance, even against your will, to mull this over. An interval to ponder your options."

"So I'm kidnapped, I'm a hostage?"

"No, Blake," Tolgate said. "They are the ones who are hostages. That family over there, your hostages."

"And they don't know...?"

"Of course not. It's their bad luck. Or maybe their good luck, that, of all the families—five hundred and ten I think the number is—that got hit by your closing of the Philadelphia factory, this group met our requirements, had what we needed."

"And what is it you needed from them?"

"Well, really, it's what you needed, Blake. They match your psychological profile, each one of them appeals to something you like about yourself, something you particularly fear or detest—no, I won't tell you what, that's what you'll start finding out once you've agreed to stay. I can tell you it's not easy for us to choose the one household that's appropriate. Though we also have to take into account availability of apartments, practicality of installing surveillance equipment on a tight schedule, you know, just like you do before deciding to rush a new item into production. But finally, I guess what clinched it was her, Roxanna. She's a natural. Just perfect. She even spoke Spanish— like your maternal grandmother, who came, if I'm not mistaken, from Granada."

"You're telling me this has something to do with my grandmother? I hardly knew her."

"She sang songs to you when you were five, six, I believe. Do you remember that? When she came to care for you when your mother became so ill?"

"I don't remember."

"And after your mother died?"

"I don't remember."

"Well, she sang those songs to your mother as well, when your mother was a child. Not that I'm saying that defined our choice. Merely added a bit of enhancement, a bonus, an extra layer of icing on the cake, so to speak. To lure you into staying."

"Well, you can lure someone else with their Spanish grandmother and lullabies and Oedipus complexes they need to work out. So you won't forfeit—a word you like so much—all you've invested. I'm sure the world is full of perverts eager to torture innocent people. You should invite Hank Granger to come and be your guest. He'd enjoy this. He'd pay six million for it. But not me. I'm out of here."

"You're out of here tomorrow, Blake. For tonight you are our guest and, if you wish to stick around for the rest of the time you have contracted, you will be our God."

What was I going to do? Insist on leaving and get beaten up by Ivan's bruising hands and end up staying the night anyway?

I was shown to my bedroom by Sandra. She had already unpacked all my things, put them in exactly the sort of order Hector has instituted at home. They had certainly studied me, grasped my quirks and habits, my tastes and eccentricities. There was a meal waiting for me, warm, my favorite pizza with goat cheese and spinach for starters, then a lovely vegetarian stew simmering on a plate, decaf capuccino mousse. Accompanied by an orchid, bursting like a fountain of white out of fresh clean water. And chamomile tea—made by my own Company, sent out by the very factory where you work, Roxanna.

"So you can sleep well," Sandra said. "No caffeine."

"I'll sleep well," I told her, and I meant it, I really thought that, somehow, just having soaked up your presence, Roxanna, would do it, free me from whatever demons had been sporting with me, playing tricks with my conscience, whispering a slime of thoughts over the last three months to startle me into eternal wakefulness. Yes, I thought I would sleep like a baby, return to Houston the next day, normalize my functions and my behavior, kiss my Thomas and my small Georgina with a light heart once again. I told myself that I had effectively banished this nonsense about a seed of evil growing inside the hidden core of my being. Tolgate had handed me the possibility of really lacerating and mangling lives and I had virtuously turned my back on his offer.

But sleep did not come. I switched off the lamp and stared up at the darkness and thought of you, Roxanna. I wondered what you were doing, how long you had managed to endure in that uncomfortable position of prayer while all around you chaos swirled, the hullabaloo of your parents arguing over who was responsible for the mess you were all in, which of the two had encouraged Ned to gamble when he was a child saying it was okay, who had invited mad Fred and his repulsive lame arm to stick around, while Jason bounced a ball inside and outside your starlet legs and dribbled around you and Ned lit up a joint as if he didn't give a fuck that he had squandered all that money on the horses. We never should have left Puerto Rico, your mom said, and your dad, and who's to blame for that, huh?, who couldn't stand working with flowers? And you, Roxanna, how could you stay calm in the midst of that havoc? How could I myself learn to stay calm in the middle of this sea of thoughts rocking me, swamping me into open-eyed vigilance? I wanted to witness, to siphon up, your next move. I wanted to learn from you. I wanted to say good-bye.

I wandered into the control room.

The cameras came on automatically. Sonia materialized out of the shadows. Tolgate and Ivan and his boys were nowhere to be seen. But they could see me: somebody in another room had to be registering my every quiver on their own machine, every shudder, every tic.

I looked for you.

You were in your room, Roxanna, on your bed. You had gotten rid of Jason, sent him off to slumber in the living room—a different camera picked up his tousled dark head peeping out of a sleeping bag on the couch—leaving you alone with—

"Who's that?"

Sonia told me it was Johnny. She could flash his life history for me if I wanted, when I wanted, but what mattered for now was his current status: Roxanna's boyfriend.

I didn't ask if he was your lover. It was clear that you'd done it with him many times over, were about to do it again tonight. Though you were, as usual, in no hurry. Teaching him the Spanish word for each herb, each leaf, you would soon be teaching him the word for each part of that body I will never touch. He was impatient, of course, but by now knew who was calling the shots, would let him come inside when everything was ready, when your juices said yes, when you were both well lubricated.

"It's always like this," Sonia said. "She takes her time. Teaches him to take his time. Time is running out, the patients say to her in the factory ward, exasperated because she never seems to hurry. She turns to them with that smile," and it was as if Sonia were in love with you, Roxanna, as if she would have done anything to trade places with avid Johnny, have your hand guiding her lingering hand as the fingers sifted together through the powder of bushes, the sweet bark of trees, "and do you know what Roxanna says? Time isn't running out. Time is always there. You're the one who's running out, running away, running too fast. Ease up. Grow like the grass. Time is the one thing nobody can take from us. That's what she says."

I watched for a while, waited for the moment when you cleared away the herbs, stashed them in the medicine kit. I watched Johnny's eyes watch you, saw you wend your way back to the bed and those fingers of yours drifting through his hair as if they were a clear stream, those fingers still tasting of the mix of mint and palmetto and St. John's wort. Then he introduced them into his mouth and sucked them one by one as if they were candy, took them out all wet and brought them down to his shirt, posed them on the top button, left the fingers there so that you could begin to unclasp it, and then, instead of going farther down right away to the next button, that hand like a bird, like a breeze, like the wake of a canoe in a lagoon, scraped the surface of his exposed dark chest, went up to the hollow in the neck, kept rising to the mouth again, your eyes were closed and I knew that you had memorized his chin and his thick lips and then your lips were on his and then again the same ritual, up toward the hair and he waited to take you to his mouth again and I said to Sonia:

"Have them stop."

"How?"

"How should I know? Just make them stop."

Sonia went to a computer screen, clicked the mouse on an icon.

"My instructions, Mr. Blake, are that you make the decisions, all of them. What happens to your family has to be your masterpiece, not mine."

"What are my options? Resources?"

Everything could be bought, she said. She began a long litany: fire department, drunken neighbors, the police...

"The police," I said. "How soon can they get here?"

"Soon. But what is it you want them to do? Arrest them both? Harass another member of the family in the next room so she and Johnny are interrupted for a while? Knock on the door with the pretext they're looking for some criminal? A drug bust? That's the easiest thing to arrange for someone like Johnny. But you're the one who has to take the lead, Mr. Blake."

Time was running out. The thought burst into my mind with all its irony. What would you have said, Roxanna, if you'd known that my hurry originated in wanting to prove you wrong: Time is the one thing others control, that you don't control if you don't have the money. Wanted you to know that you should have rushed, speeded toward a quick in and out, a hasty orgasm, because I wasn't going to let you have all the time in the world. I wasn't going to let you be in command of your own time.

"I want him arrested," I said. "Have them... have the police book him for drugs, slip some cocaine into his pockets."

"It's already happening," she said. She spoke into a microphone. "You heard what he wants, Ivan. And he wants it now."

I was surprised at how soon they managed it. Not more than five minutes could have passed. You had his shirt off by then, Roxanna, he had you down to your bra, his fingers and your fingers already interlaced—and then the cops broke down the door. I'd never seen a door being broken down. Only in films. A violent kick splits the wood, sends it flying, makes the most jarring noise. And then they were swarming all over you, both of you, guns swinging wildly, hands doing their business.

"I didn't say they were supposed to paw her," I complained to Sonia.

"You need to be specific, Mr. Blake. But don't worry. They won't arrest Roxanna. You do need to understand, however, that you can't always determine every side effect. You'll learn."

"You been working at this for a long time?"

"I'm not authorized to discuss my private life or my past, Mr. Blake. How long do you wish this Johnny fellow held?"

I told her that I'd let her know when I wanted him released. Not to do anything to him. No beatings. No rough stuff at all. Was that clear?

"Anything else?"

I watched your tears, Roxanna. I wanted to stop them. I wanted those tears to go on. On and on so I could wipe them clean.

"Keep me informed of what happens to him. Hey, where does she think she's going?"

"I suppose she's going to try to spring her lover boy out of jail."

And I knew, without a moment's hesitation, I knew that I couldn't let that happen. You had to be free of him to carry out the plan that was beginning to take shape, uncoil, inside me. So I could test you, test you and perhaps save myself.

"Make sure she can't get in to see him."

I saw you begin to dress. I saw that you still did not hurry. I had savaged your existence, arrested your Johnny, broken down your family's door, and you were floating as always like a lazy bee through life. Well, we'd see if that was how it would be, if you could resist me, we'd see what the next month of trials would bring.

"Sleep well, Mr. Blake."

Not only sleep well. Oversleep. Ten hours. When I awoke, you had already gone to work, Roxanna. Your mother wasn't around either, or your kid brother. But the rest of them were lolling around, the menfolk, your no-good brother and that father of yours who was calling in sick and that burping Fred with his dangling arm, they were sitting at a card table—at nine in the morning, dealing them out, blackjack they were playing, chugging the beer as if it were water.

I had breakfast while I studied their movements, had Sandra call up their histories on the computer.

"How is she taking it?"

"Who?"

"Roxanna. With her boyfriend busted. How is she holding up?"

"She prayed for him this morning, prayed for several of her patients, bounced off full of cheerfulness. The girl believes in the American system, thinks justice will be done."

"Will it?"

"That depends on you." It was Dr. Tolgate. Coming by for our morning therapy session.

No couch. Just the two of us, face-to-face, though his chair was more comfortable than mine, a swiveler, leather arm pads, nice.

"I don't know why I feel so energized," I said to him. "I should be feeling miserable. What I did last night is the worst thing I've ever done in my life."

"You're sure?"

"Of course I'm sure. I don't do that sort of thing. Ever. It's—it's unthinkable."

"Not anymore," Dr. Tolgate said. "You thought it into existence, it was inside. Maybe you needed it to come out, bring it into the open air, look at it."

"Like vomit," I said.

"If that's the metaphor you want to use. Maybe there are angels inside you as well. Maybe they'll also come out. Look at it this way: How else can you get to know who you are, what you really want? Remember. So far you haven't really hurt anybody. You can let Johnny go right now, our happy couple can be fornicating in front of your hungry eyes this very night. Or you can wait till the end of the month."

I've waited till the end of my month, as you have had occasion to see and suffer, Roxanna mine. But your Johnny's going to be free soon, just as I promised you under my breath that first night. I said to myself, to your hazel eyes and your skin the color of a dark moon in the night,

I said, I'm doing this for her good. To cure myself, yes, but I'll end up doing more good than bad, better than the next guy who comes along, someone who will take my place if I abandon this therapy. I cast myself as saving you from the likes of Hank Granger, blocking someone like that pervert from taking over your life. First some bad luck, to be sure, to make the ending sweeter. I'll shower them with gifts, I promised myself. Eventually. All in good time.

It's all gone according to the game plan I conceived that first full day I spent in the clinic. I had counted on this being a vacation, but it turned out to be hard work. Like laying out an ad campaign: deadlines, twists and turns, manipulation of images, except that here I was maneuvering and deploying real people in real time and real space. Almost like designing a new factory, opening a new spa in Madagascar. Exhilarating, Roxanna, I hate to admit it. Admit it, Tolgate said. It'll do you good. It's fun, he said.

"It is fun," I said to myself, say to myself whenever doubts begin to prowl inside. But the point is that the therapy is working and how can I argue with a good night's sleep, the fact that I am being cured, drop by drop, by what I am doing to you. The only night when I couldn't sleep, when the migraine started to crawl back under my temples, last night. I called Tolgate at around three in the morning.

"Normal reaction," he said. His favorite words. "You're about to depart, ready for the final act. You've been obsessed with this woman and will never see her again after tomorrow. But tonight's just a bump in the road. Think how successful, after all, your venture has been, right?"

Yes. Everything has proceeded according to the script I improvised with Sonia's assistance while you were away at work that first day, Roxanna. At the very time you were helping my employees at the factory heal, so that they could more efficiently produce cereals and vitamins, special teas and magically named pills, oils, and ointments, all destined to calm the nerves of our America, during those same hours, I was letting my feverish imagination loose on your so-American family, calming my own nerves with every gambit and ruse I could craft.

It's been like a dream.

That first morning, that's when I decided to corral you, with the same easygoing diligence you flaunted at me, patiently drive you into a corner, force you to realize that I exist, this shadow here on the other side. Help you reach a point where your sudden streak of bad luck would no longer seem arbitrary. If you could discern the elegance of my strategy, contemplate your life from outside it as I do. If you could just move your beautiful butt a few feet away, to this apartment on the other side of your wall, that would be enough. Or if I could travel across this wall, penetrate this wall, penetrate the wall of your slow flesh, reach you, illuminate you as to what the grand plan was, has been, will be. The plan: Test your true inner strength by isolating you from those you love. See if your serenity foundered. See how long it would take you to curse whatever obstinate deity was raining disasters upon your family. Make you like your mother, who blames God, the whole of creation, even the flowers, for your family's fate.

I knew what I would do with each of them. Except your father. But the rest: It became clear as I debated each case with Sonia, allowed Sandra to bring up their life history on the green screen.

Jason was the easiest. This weekend a scout would "discover" him playing on the neighborhood court and sign him up for a special training camp, preprofessional, take him off to California for three, maybe more, weeks.

"He's a bit young," Sonia objected, "but we can swing it. For a month, at least, you'll be rid of his presence at home. She'll miss him."

"I think that's the point."

Equilibrium, I thought to myself: I was giving one sibling, Jason, a stab at success, because the other one was going to be my victim. I'd get Ned a job—the next day, preferably, driving a dump truck. I liked the idea of the lounging, pot-smoking, lanky brother working with that tremendous noise shaking the truck and clawing the air with its roar. I wanted a minor accident to befall him: "Can you arrange things so he goes deaf for a month?"

"You want Ned to lose his hearing for a month?"

"Only for a month. Can that be arranged?"

"I'll see," Sonia said. "Maybe blindness for a month, maybe lameness, the loss of feeling in the left leg, which would justify an operation. A fake operation, of course. Somebody used that once to get rid of a guy they wanted out of the way and it was not a half-bad idea. Easier than deafness. Did you know that Roxanna is a bit hard of hearing? So it might run in the family: if you meddle with the inner ear, this Ned guy could lose his hearing for good. Unless that's what you want? Leave a more permanent mark, a scar, on him?"

I didn't much care which of these alternatives she chose.

Had I just thought that, said that? Was that the voice of Graham Blake saying that he didn't care?

Almost unrecognizable. Almost. Also somehow familiar, this secret well of sounds I had carried within me forever and did not want to admit, drink from. It had been waiting, this voice that speaks to you, Roxanna, inside me, like a child that was born deformed and deranged and was shut away to starve by the family and survived by feeding on himself in the dark. With nobody to accompany him but his own echo in the dark, swearing he would emerge.

My voice now. And back then. That Sonia did not, does not judge. She listened attentively as I told her, by all means, to have Ned diagnosed with some strange neurological symptom—not what his sister has, whatever that might be. As long as he was out of the apartment, I told her. And also, make sure the insurance company announces to the family that this particular sickness isn't covered under the medical plan. Or fix it so that the plan has just expired, that's even more anguishing.

"You want them to think that your Company failed to pay the premiums on the medical insurance?"

"Let them take us to court. By the time they've secured a lawyer, gone through all the steps, the month will be up and they'll be told it was all a misunderstanding, a legal snafu."

"You're the boss," Sonia said.

I looked at her sharply. There seemed to be no irony in her remark. What I did notice was a certain admiration scrolling into her gray, frigid eyes, as if to say, You're the best, you're really devious, I've seen tons of patients in therapy, but you eclipse them all.

That got me warmed up. My next move would be to vandalize Silvia's lunch cart, steal her goods and her money. But wait! First get someone to impersonate a phony customer so entranced with Silvia's food that he'd offer to buy her business, lunch cart and all, set her up in a real restaurant. Of course, once the assault had happened, given that the cart was in shambles, the deal would be called off. Then, the next day, Ned's accident—that would make Silvia's loss even more disheartening and—

"You're really pouring it on, aren't you?"

"I thought you," I said to Sonia, "were supposed to be neutral in this."

"Do whatever you want, Mr. Blake," she responded. "My question isn't ethical. It's aesthetic. One catastrophe after another makes for a boring month—for them, for you, for me and Sandra. I was betting that you'd offer us all a good show."

Maybe she didn't admire me as much as I thought. Maybe it wouldn't be that easy to get her into bed.

"There will be reversals, my dear," I promised. I told her about my idea for Fred. His arm had been irreparably injured, according to his dossier, by one of the defective bottling machines for cold creams in my old factory, and he was still waiting, two years later, for his worker's compensation. So I thought I'd sweeten his life somewhat, arrange an inheritance for him. Not really endowing him with it. A letter would do, suggesting he might be the heir to a fortune left by some unknown relative, an eccentric millionaire secret aunt. Entice him out of there—and, of course give the family the hope that he would return with money to help them, return from… from Vancouver, let's say, send him across the continent. And take that withered branch of his arm with him. Arriving in Vancouver, Fred should be informed that his "aunt" has mandated a clause in the will to make sure that nobody takes advantage of him: For one whole year he cannot see or even contact anybody he has been spending time with over the last decade, isolating him from the family that offered him refuge when he was sick and lost.

Sonia noted this down, made no comment, didn't meet my eyes.

"I'll make it up to him, don't worry."

"I'm not worried," Sonia said. "It's not my treatment and not my money. If you want to make it up to him, it'll cost you. Extra. Those are my instructions."

"I'll make it up to him," I repeated.

"How about Roxanna?"

"She's the only one I won't touch. Only the people she loves, who love her."

"And Bud?"

I hadn't yet made up my mind about your father, Roxanna. Precisely because I disliked him so intensely, I held off my desire to crush him, inspired by a certain generosity of spirit that my mother taught me before she died, that my father encouraged actively, perhaps because he had a vague Quaker heritage. He once took me down to his club at the Union League, walked me up the ample marble stairs to a room overlooking the street. He planted me in front of the window and waited and then said, suddenly, "Let's go." He had spotted two beggars, mooching on the corner. "Let's visit," he said.

One was a teenage girl, pretty, relatively clean, with an enchanting voice. That voice! I can still remember her there, singing on that corner. Nearby was a mess of a man, bedraggled, stoned out of his wits, smelling of shit and the acrid exhalation of cheap wine, begging for a coin, molesting the tourists and businessmen who hurried by him. "One hundred dollars," my dad said, taking out the bill. It was crisp and caustic and new. "Who do we give this to?" I pointed at the girl and he shook his head. "She'll get the next ten handouts. He won't get a one, not one. He horrifies us, horrifies you, and that's why you need to give him this bill. That's true charity: to dispense money to those who don't deserve it."

But let me confess, Roxanna, that this was not the only reason to help your undeserving dad. It would be interesting, I thought, to promote him from just an ordinary guard to head of security at the factory, because it would unleash tremendous tensions at home. To have him doing better day after day while the rest of the household—with the exceptions of the absent Jason and the absent Fred—went down the drain. I wondered how you'd deal, Roxanna of the always calm body and mind, with a grieving mother and an exultant father who were already at each other's throats all day long, a battle that got on my nerves and had to get on yours, had to be affecting you. Or would affect you if I exacerbated those strains day by day with tiny surgical interventions. Two armies at war being secretly commanded by the same five-star general. Like playing poker with myself as a child, knowing the cards my rival held, cheating him, always winning, I always won every game.

That decision to grace and upgrade your father, Roxanna, turned out to be premature. No sooner did you glide through the door that afternoon and he looked at you as if you were his prey, kissed you on the mouth, in front of your mother, winking at both your brothers, than I began to have second thoughts. But I didn't change my mind right away: I let you discreetly disengage, begin to unpack the groceries you'd brought for dinner, inform them all you had been unable to see Johnny but had retained a good lawyer who had promised to beat this ridiculous trumped-up charge. Fortunately your brother asked the lawyer's name, so I was able to pass it on to Sandra. "Have somebody offer the guy a couple of fat corporate white-collar crimes," I counseled her. "Just make sure he postpones any work on Johnny."

Maybe if you'd known that I was already hatching that scheme for torpedoing your lawyer, you wouldn't have helped your mother so joyfully with the meal. The way you minced the bell peppers, peeled the cucumber clean and white with your darkened hands, lay the lettuce out so that the juice from the tomatoes could be captured in its leaves, everything perfect, nothing rushed—and then excused yourself, found a corner where you could meditate and pray.

You seemed to prefer, seemed to even love, doing those exercises in the middle of the noise, Spanish catcalls, Caribbean music, everything swirling around you. As you settled into serenity, concentrating on your Johnny, perhaps on each one of the humbled men and women you had tended to during the day, drifting out to them, following up your prescriptions and massages and balms with an imaging of their face and wounds, your father came up from behind you and began to mock you, bringing his hands together in an exaggerated Buddha-like pose, moving his hips in an obscene little jig, rolling his eyes upward to a heaven he obviously didn't believe in—all to the great hilarity of everyone else, even Jason, even Silvia. Your mother went so far as to come up to her husband and begin to rhumba with him and soon they were all cavorting around you, making you out to be a fool.

"Fire him," I heard my voice say. "Fire the bastard."

"You're sure?" Sonia asked.

"This Bud guy must go out to bars," I said. "Does he? Does he go out to bars?" She nodded. "Have somebody set him up with drinks, ply him with as many as he wants. And that fool Fred as well. Then have whoever's providing the booze suggest they go and insult me, the owner of the Company, throw stones at the factory Bud is supposed to be protecting. Have him caught by his own mates, the night security guards."

"How many people have you fired in your life, Blake?"

It was Tolgate. He had come in without my noticing it, perhaps he'd been here all this time, ever since you'd come home from work. How long had he been watching my performance?

"I don't like firing people," I said, without turning around. "I can't tell you how careful I've been about that. If you know so much about me, Doctor, you know this: I've gone out of my way to keep jobs. It's my first priority. Better to get rid of corporate perks, bonuses, before terminating someone. That's been our policy. Expand. Grow. Hire,

hire, hire. Every time I've had to sack one person, I make sure I hire two others. Firing is the temporary situation. Just like now. I'm booting Bud, but at the end of the month he'll be back at his job."

"You don't need to justify your actions, Blake."

"I'm not—"

"Yes you are. You want my approval. Fuck my approval. Expand, you said. But you didn't. In this case, you didn't, did you? You closed down the high-tech plant where half this family worked and you may have to close down the older one as well."

You were heading for the bathroom, Roxanna, and it seemed the wrong moment to get into a protracted discussion with Tolgate about economics. What did he know about business, with his puny company? Was he part of the Fortune 500? Did he go to Davos every February? I decided to cut him short.

"Listen, Tolgate, I'm not closing down shit. It's a transitory thing, okay? The Asian crisis has brought down the demand, created some financial turbulence, our e-commerce has not met expectations, so we had to pause and wait, but as soon as—"

You were disrobing, taking off your blouse first, then your dress, about to let your panties fall to your feet, fling off—slowly, slowly—your bra and reveal yourself naked to me for the first time.

Tolgate stepped in front of me, shielded your body with his. The intensity in his voice did not allow me to ignore it, forced me to look straight at him, miss the moment when you were finally unclothed and stepped into the shower. Over his voice I could hear yours, humming a Spanish song, something about a *paloma*, over his voice the splash of the water on your shoulders, down your back, along your legs.

"I don't want to hear about Asia," Tolgate said. "Or oversupply. Or expansion into bigger plants because prices are going up. Or idling those plants later because prices, of course, then fall. Cycles of boom and bust bore me. The International Monetary Fund bores me. The Russian debt. The Latin American miracle. Blah-blah-blah. The e-mail revolution or evolution or devolution, the virtual whatever the disembodied fuck it is. I don't give a damn that a day will come when, in order to save your Company, you'll probably give the order to throw your enchanting Roxanna out on the street. Where she'll peddle whatever she can peddle, like all of us who weren't born with a factory in our laps. Or met a woman who was a bioengineering genius. None of that matters."

He shifted because he saw I was trying to peep around him, I wasn't listening as I should have been. Tolgate placed his body even closer to mine, like a screen blotting out the rest of the world.

"The only thing that matters here is what you feel, to get in touch with the real you. Not something theoretical. Not something your dad or your mom wanted you to be. Your emotions. Your desires. You want to talk economics? Here's a market—right there on that other side— that you can control. Here you demand, Blake, and they supply, your family supplies. Here you produce and they automatically consume. You cook, they eat. Or, if you'd rather turn the image around, you eat them. Savor them, chew them, gulp them down, digest them, shit them. With no public power to counteract your private needs, no press, no competition, no regulatory agency, no lobbying from public interest groups to restrain your growth, no congressman to soften up with campaign funds. You have a monopoly on that family over there. Understood? They can't protect themselves, can't elevate tariffs, delay exchange-rate convertibility, blame you for safety hazards. Blake, you're free. Nobody will ever know what you did, what you didn't do. So no more justifying your conduct. That's a Graham Blake you left outside the door. He may be waiting for you in a month's time. Or he may have vanished. That's what we're here to find out. But he's had you for forty-three years. All I'm asking for is thirty days."

Now he stepped away. There you were, just out of the shower, entirely at the disposal of my eyes. Without looking at your body himself, Tolgate gestured toward you. "Don't hold back, Blake. Something's been seething inside you, you've been suppressing it, that's what bites at you, not letting you rest."

You were toweling with such subdued abandon, so gloriously dedicated to your skin, each of your toes, and suddenly I had the urge to hurt you, smash in your face, hear you whimper, puncture your autonomy, and I was scared, Roxanna, I didn't like what I was allowing to slither forth, I luxuriated in these thoughts so immensely and hated how I relished them and—

"So that's who I am?" I said to Tolgate, the old Graham Blake who had supposedly been left outside the door said to him. "This horrible thing? This primal urge to harm people? And all the rest is just a veneer that we can wash off as if it were the day's dirt?"

"I said a deep part of you, not the deepest part. Go for it and maybe you'll find something underneath what you're doing, something deeper, more essentially you. Go for it. Don't hold back."

I haven't held back, Roxanna.

I've gone through with my agenda, my strategy of encirclement, as if you were a consumer who had to be sold on a product, had a product rammed down her reluctant throat. Me. I'm the product. Rammed down your throat day after day like a secret cough. Like a virus down your brown slack throat to see if you'll sicken. But nothing I've done has shocked you out of your cheerfulness, your belief in the American dream, the goodness of man and the healthiness of God and the benevolence of the universe and the glory of flowers.

And today I gave up, I recognized my defeat. I reversed it all, am about to prove you right. You're the one who has convinced and converted me, your quiet and generous resolution in the midst of the plagues and voids and absences I've visited upon you has forced me to pass on to Sonia this very afternoon an alternative finale to your story with which, in spite of Tolgate's admonitions, I had always been furtively justifying my behavior to myself during this last month. I'm sending you this good-bye present, Roxanna: a happy ending.

Bud gets his job back, along with a promotion. Jason comes home with a scholarship and a promise from the basketball training camp that if he finishes high school with honors, they'll continue to assist him. The police have found the culprits who shattered Silvia's business, a couple of rich kids who will pay through the nose to avoid prosecution, and she can buy herself a modest restaurant, a real one. Fred should be back with some money—not as much as he expected, but still enough for some fancy meals, a tidy sum to get him started on a newsstand, a perfect occupation for a one-armed man. And I'll look into the matter of his compensation for that accident when I'm back in control in Houston. As for Ned's paralysis or lameness or whatever the fuck I inoculated him with, it will be mysteriously over—as mysteriously as it began. Maybe the suffering he's been through will cure him of his addiction to gambling.

"And Johnny," I say to Sonia. "Have him released right away."

"Right away?"

"Today. Now. I want to see Roxanna's face when her prayers are answered."

"You want to see them make love?"

"Yes. I want to see them make love because I allowed it."

"I'll see what I can do."

Sonia left with my orders a few hours ago. She's grown exuberant, less tight-assed, more sensual, as the days have gone by. Tonight, after I've watched you and your Johnny make out, after you've exhausted yourselves on your bed, it'll be my turn to say good-bye to Sonia, glad that I managed to seduce her. We'll step outside the range of the perpetually red blinking lights of the cameras that are always recording my every exploit, we'll cheat those devices and steal our last pleasures, our own little going-away party.

It was a smart choice: to bed my keeper, the woman who holds the keys to my kingdom, who knows all the ropes. The one person who could foil Ivan if need be. I've always known how to do that, Roxanna, and if we were ever to meet in the real world, I could charm you as well. Look at frigid Sonia: I made her more devoted to me than to Tolgate and the salary he pays her. In a mere month. And under the watchful eye of ugly Sandra, the Doctor himself, his henchmen. Look at how Sonia's gone off to do my bidding.

But now. But now. Now. Now Sonia enters the room and by the shuffling, dejected way she walks, by her pale face, I realize something is wrong, something has gone terribly wrong.

She stutters something. I can't make it out. "I... I..."

She... she... What?

"I can't get them to obey."

"What do you mean?"

"They say you've been too capricious, *arbitrary*'s the word they used. Gone overboard, over-reached yourself. So they can't... Jason, yes. Fred. That should be no problem, they'll be back by tomorrow, but the other requests, they're not sure. The situation certainly won't be resolved right away, as you asked, certainly not before you leave. The reversal is too sudden, they say. You've made too many demands."

There was something else, Roxanna. Something she wasn't telling me, didn't want to admit.

"But Tolgate said that I could do whatever I wanted, he assured me—"

"Tolgate always says that. To make sure the patient won't hold back, telling himself that later he can effortlessly improve the condition of the people he's screwed over. But Tolgate doesn't always deliver."

"What? This is a breach of contract, of confidence, this is—What else? There's something else."

And then, Roxanna, right now, just as the phone rings in your apartment, just as you are shaken out of your prayers and leap toward the phone that rings like a cat dying in the next room, just as you pick up the receiver, Sonia reveals to me that—

"He's dead," Sonia says. "Johnny. This morning. He committed suicide. Or maybe... They didn't want to tell us, have kept it under wraps. Maybe they gave him a beating and he... They're covering something up, I think, figuring out how to deal with the stink. It's my guess that that's why they don't want to honor your other requests. They're pissed with you. Blame you for the mess."

Johnny's dead? It can't be, it can't be, Roxanna. I won't let it happen, I—it can't be true, it—

But it's true. You're finding out how true it is right now, Roxanna, my poor Roxanna. The phone is telling you it's true, who is it there on the other side of the line? Johnny's mother, Johnny's jailer, Johnny's ghost—he is dead, your scream tells me so, your sobs tell me he's dead. I killed him, I killed the poor son of a bitch, your body in convulsions tells me that it's my fault. And there's nobody to embrace you, I've organized this loneliness for you, this murderous sorrow for you, this empty comfortless apartment. I've banished the whole lot of them and ship-wrecked you, left you by yourself to face my handiwork, my month's labor of love. I have finally got through to you, ravaged your peace, quickened your gait, jump-started you out of your lazy dance of life.

Because now my eyes follow you, my Roxanna mine, into the bath-room, you rush there as if possessed by a serpentlike speed and shake out all those tablets—No! Don't do it, don't. They spill over your hand onto the floor, you are down on your knees like a pig scrounging for its supper, scrambling them into your mouth, drinking in death as if it were a glass of water, splashing them down into your gullet with the greedy water of the faucet spurting all over your body, so recklessly that I almost can't see you doing it. I press a button, the camera zooms in for the close-up, suddenly goes on the blink, fuzzes, crackles, comes back on, you—

"My God! She's going to kill herself."

I turn to Sonia. She does nothing, says nothing. Her gray eyes, her close-cropped hair, her breasts wanting to rise out of the tightly-clad sweater. Nothing.

I shake her, try to shake sense, urgency into her. "Do something," I say to her.

"It's your family. Your call. If you want me to dial nine-one-one, just tell me. But all hell will break loose. We'll be investigated, they're bound to ask how come we—"

And then I know what I want her to do, I know why I've been playing with her life like I've been playing with yours, Roxanna, how I anticipated Sonia could repay the panting orgasms I've coaxed out of her hard, cold body: I want her to help me cross over. That's been my real dream, my secret plan, all this month. Break the one rule that can't be broken, go beyond the limit that Tolgate has decreed for God, for me, for all his patients.

And she agrees. She points out that this means we could all be prosecuted, but Sonia will do it as I knew she would, as I told myself she would as I slipped in and out of her body thinking of your warmth, Roxanna, plowing her for your benefit, so that I could save you, undo this net of terror I've cast over your existence.

"Ivan!" Sonia's curt voice speaks into the microphone while I watch you slump down on the bathroom floor, Roxanna, your lovely legs awkwardly askew, twisted, contorted. "Ivan, there's an emergency. I need you to go right away to the police station. Take the men with you. Yes, all of them. Make sure Johnny's father doesn't get his body back. Yes, I said everybody. I know your instructions. Fuck your instructions. Okay, okay. If you've got to leave somebody, leave Benjy, then. Downstairs, right. Guarding the other apartment."

She stops speaking, turns to me.

"I'll take care of Benjy." And then: "You realize, Blake, that I'm out of a job. There'll be reprisals. Tolgate is merciless. I hope you—"

"My God, woman, we'll discuss your financial future once we've fixed this mess. I'll provide for you. I always take care of the people who serve me."

"Service night and day, that's me, Your Majesty," Sonia says, wisecracking as if we were in some Hollywood action flick where the stars give themselves time to make supposedly witty remarks in the middle of mayhem and explosions. But she can make all the ironic comments she wants as long as what I'm seeing is true: She is opening, she's really opening the magic door. I haven't been through it in a whole month, have imagined but never seen the hallway we're going down, always visualized a guard in place, two of them, but now, thanks to Sonia, there's not one in sight. They're all hustling off on a fool's errand to the police station where poor Johnny's body is. I don't want to think about him now, only about you, Roxanna—only about this corridor, this elevator button Sonia is pressing, this elevator lurching downward: All of this has been outside my apartment the entire month, waiting for me, waiting for this moment when I leave the building that has housed me and my sophomoric soap-opera schemes.

No guard here either. All so remarkably easy. I should have tried it before. If I had made the attempt a few days ago, and touched your hand, Roxanna—that's really all I needed, to feel skin against skin, to ruffle, jar, touch your life, not penetrate, no need to fuck, just to jump the barriers—that would have been enough, I'd have given the order for Johnny's release in time for him to survive, he'd be alive now and you, you wouldn't be lying there like my mother when she—

I don't want to think about this, just want to sprint behind Sonia as she weaves her way through the passersby on this ordinary Philadelphia street, around the corner, along the block, to the apartment building behind ours, your building stuck to mine like two dogs in heat making love.

"Here," says Sonia, handing me a key. "It's eight-E."

"How about you?"

She nods toward the darkened hallway inside the building. Not as run-down as I had imagined from... "Big Benjy is in there," Sonia says. "I'll entertain him. He's got the hots for me. Calls me his Snow Princess. Wait fifteen—no, twenty seconds—before sneaking in."

I do as I'm told. For the first time in a month, obeying orders instead of handing them out. In Sonia's hands like you were in mine, Roxanna.

Fifteen seconds later—hold on, Roxanna, hold on, I'm on my way—I carefully sidle into the building, across the foyer, find the elevator. To one side, at the start of the stairwell, I can make out Sonia's silhouette, a man's bulk leaning over her, Benjy getting his big hands on her breasts, his lips on his Snow Princess's mouth—and I'm in the elevator, rising up, up, eight floors to you, to apartment 8E.

The key fits wonderfully, miraculously, magically, I'm inside, I hardly have the time to register that I'm seeing the apartment for real, from here, I don't have time to wonder how my body might look from the vantage point I have been using all these weeks, how the cameras that have been at my beck and call must be registering my rush across this room I know so well, into the bedroom I have memorized through my glass partition and my videotapes, into this bathroom, into your inner sanctum, Roxanna, where I first saw your body stepping out of the shower.

It's you. It's really you on the floor, gasping for breath. Until now, I realize with a shock, I wasn't entirely convinced you were real. You had to be a dream Tolgate had concocted, a film he had shot on a set—that suspicion aching into me, that you were too good to be true, too perfect a fit for my desires, too close to what I had always most wanted from a woman, from life, what Jessica couldn't give me, what Natasha hasn't.

And now you're dying, my Roxanna mine, really mine, because I can touch you, take you in my arms, force your eyes open, your mouth open, force you to cough out, spit, vomit what is churning in the dark cavern of your stomach, put my mouth to your mouth and breathe in, breathe out into the stale, rancid air of this bathroom, breathe in again, returning to you the life I stole. You're coming back, now you're awake, gagging, desperately whooping oxygen and hope into those sweet lungs. And you look into my eyes.

Roxanna, you look into my eyes.

Straight into me. No glass between us, no one-way mirrors, no tricks, no wall, no cameras. Face-to-face. Deep into me. Like a mother to a child, I think, I cannot help but think. Like a mother to a child who was lost and now is found.

And I know that I'm a good man. I know that you see who I really am. Someone who can play with others, who can do terrible things, but also me, this sinner who can find in himself the strength and the courage to repent and accept what he's done, who will spend the rest of his life repairing that damage.

I will confess everything, right now I will confess it all. And you will forgive me.

Your eyes tell me that I will be forgiven.

THREE

"So you don't mind if we ask you some questions, miss?"

"Why should I mind?" she says. "I've already told you people everything there is to tell about the suicide."

"Not to us, miss. And, besides, my friend here and me, we tend to ask other things."

"Yeah, that's right. We belong to a different unit, you know—specializing in other things."

"But you won't mind if we ask about the circumstances surrounding what seems to be your friend's suicide, miss, right? We'll just start this camera rolling…"

"Seems to be?" she says. "You have doubts? I hadn't heard that anybody had doubts. That's not what your colleagues at the police department said when—"

"What my colleague here is saying is that you can never rule out anything when somebody dies like that in mysterious circumstances."

"Yes, it's always good, as my colleague says, to try and clear everything up. Ask some more questions, you know, if you don't mind."

"Go ahead," she says.

"Because the door was locked from the inside when you got there that day, when your friend, she… if I'm not mistaken, when she…? Your boyfriend wasn't with you that day, right, miss?"

"I've told you this so many times," she says, "that I—"

"Not us, you've told somebody else, but not us, miss."

"What happened to my *comadre*…" she says. "Well, she was upset. They'd been interviewing her, some experts, efficiency experts, streamline experts they called themselves. They asked me questions too, at my job, all of us. She'd been having some trouble at her factory, making some slipups, mistakes. She worked in labeling, you know, with all this equipment that operates so quickly that you only have a split second to make sure the right label is on the right package, and the factory had to recall a small shipment of the Soothing Tea series. She'd programmed the machine to paste some of the labels on Energy Brew instead."

"Doesn't sound like a big deal to me."

"That's what I felt," she says. "So some customer thinks he'll have a good night's sleep and instead he's up until morning all bleary-eyed and he sends in a complaint, some asshole *idiota* has the time to sit down and write a letter about it, when he should be celebrating that we shook him up a bit and made him face his image in the mirror one whole blessed night, lucky man."

"But management reprimanded your friend…"

"Yes," she says, "so she was *aprehensiva*, and she came out of the interview really raw, angry, *con coraje*, you know, what right do those bastards—"

"They were men?"

"So she told me, yes, two men," she says, "not a man and a woman like with me, when they interviewed me later. They asked her all sorts of questions about her private life, taped her, what she liked, what she hated, things that had no bearing on her job. They even asked her about me."

"About you, miss?"

"About me," she says. "Is there anything wrong with that? Because my boyfriend thought it was strange. And she did too."

"Your friend Evangelina?"

"Yes," she says.

"You're sure that was her name, miss? Evangelina? Because we've been given information that she might have been using another name."

"Her name was Evangelina," she says.

"She was a bit… high-strung, your friend, right?"

"A bit," she says. "Not so strange, to be like that. Like my mother. My mother got so angry that she refused to answer any of their questions, left the questionnaire blank, *qué les importa?*, mamá said, what do they care, why should they know these things, whether I like flowers or not, how we came to the States, what your favorite color is, girl?"

"They wanted to know what your favorite color was, miss?"

"My favorite color," she says, "and my favorite song and my favorite movie."

"Your favorite movie."

"Yeah, what is your favorite movie?"

"You promise not to laugh?" she says. "*Snow White*. Everybody laughs when I say that—but I love it, that song 'Someday My Prince Will Come,' I just love that song."

"To get back to Evangelina, or whatever her name is, and why she was so upset… if you don't mind."

"Evangelina felt they were messing with her life," she says. "And I go, wait a minute, take it easy, they're here to help, *mujer*, they've been hired to find ways of saving your job. But she wouldn't listen—don't try to cheer me up, I'm tired of you always trying to cheer everybody up, always thinking the best of everybody! *Hasta cuándo!* Hold on, I said, hold on, girl, we—We should strike, she said. Go on strike before they close this fucker down—begging your pardon, but those were her words, I don't use them—she said management was going to close it down, you see, wait and watch. She was a hothead. Puerto Ricans are like that. Into politics. Not like me. I'm always trying to get people to agree, get along together, maybe because I don't like conflict. My friend Georgia says it's because I come from a home where the mother and the father are always going at each other all day long, but I don't think so. I've learned to zone out, pretend nothing's happening, nobody's yapping around me. Which doesn't mean I can't fight if I have to, if my back's to the wall. But fighting should be a last resort, like I told Evangelina."

"So you disagreed with Evangelina on that, miss?"

"You had words with her?"

"No," she said, "I understood her. Evangelina wanted to do something drastic because she felt she had lost control, she felt they'd taken her life away from her, as if they'd stripped her of her clothes, but it's worse when you strip people of their secrets."

"She had secrets?"

"Everybody has secrets," she says.

"Now, this friend of yours, Evangelina, you're sure that's her name, this friend of yours, you've known her since when?"

"Since my first day in school," she says.

"And you were ten, right? Just arrived here in the country? Didn't know any English?"

"She was sitting next to me," she says. "Maybe they sat her next to me because she knew Spanish and could help me. And she did, she was the best friend I've ever had."

"But you noticed something wrong with her."

"Wrong with her?" she says.

"You thought she looked sick."

"That's what our notes say: 'Evangelina looked sick and I felt really sorry for her.'"

"And that's when you decided to steal flowers, bring her a flower the next day."

"Not just her," she says. "Not just Evangelina. They all looked sick, pale, unhappy, all the kids in the school. They all needed cheering up, it seemed to me."

"So you stole the flowers."

"I didn't think of it as stealing," she says.

"Borrowing, huh? You thought of it as borrowing, right?"

"Yes," she says. "I thought I'd return two flowers for each flower that I took from the shops that afternoon. When I became rich and famous, you know how kids are. Look, I was just ten and back home I'd—maybe I should explain this to you so that you don't get the wrong impression."

"Maybe you should explain, miss. Seeing as this suicide thing doesn't seem clear either."

"It's a sort of long story," she says.

"We don't mind."

"That's right, we have tons of time. Be our guest."

"It's difficult for people here to get it," she says, "but I—look, you see this. You know what this is? It's a saltshaker. I brought it with me when I came here from my country with my mother and my elder brother. I still carry it around even if I no longer use it the way I did back then, the way I had planned to when I arrived. I didn't know what the States would be like, except they'd told me it was a big city we were flying to, but I thought there'd be fields, so that when I took a shortcut home or to school, I could just grab a tomato and sprinkle it with salt and eat it, just like that, and the onions, especially the young green onions just peeping out from the earth. You've never had them, like that, *cebollitas tiernas*?"

"Can't say that I have, miss."

"We're city people, miss, I think you can tell."

"Well, I feel sorry for you then," she says, "begging your pardon. A few days after the *cebollitas* have made their appearance on this earth, they're like everything newborn, full of life and very tender. Never? With salt. So good. But here in Philadelphia, well, it was—so sad.

There were no fields, no onions to be snatched, no snacks on my way to anywhere. Everything was boxed up, including the flowers. Which I couldn't believe. It's like the flowers were silently screaming their sorrow at being locked up. It must be terrible to be locked up, to—like being back underground again. I don't like to think about that, about being—"

"We understand, miss. There's no need to get upset."

"Anybody's who lost a friend like you have…"

"But you were trying to explain why you stole those flowers, miss. Maybe…"

"Yes," she says. "Flowers were always, well, free, you know. The first ten years of my life were spent with flowers, gathering them, always trying to find one that was different. I think I started to do that back in Catalina, where I was born, because of my mamá's family. I knew before I could even walk that they didn't speak to us, to my mother, to my brother, to me, that my grandparents, aunts, uncles, all those cousins, made believe we didn't exist, my mamá had said it was useless to even try to contact them—we have to keep our *dignidad, niña*, it's the only riches the poor have got, our dignity—but I didn't listen to her, even when I was a *chiquita* this size, I knew what I wanted."

"That's always a good thing, miss."

"Yes. Not everybody knows what they want, miss. And you were—what age were you at about that time?"

"Back in Catalina?" she says. "Six, probably, when I began to leave a different flower each morning on the doorstep of my grandparents' house and the houses belonging to my uncles and aunts."

"They must have known it was you, miss."

"Not at first," she says. "I would watch from behind a gigantic magnolia tree in the plaza and see my grandmother open the door and find an iris there or an *azucena*, or at other times a specially bright *amapola*, and orchids, of course, because Catalina was famous for its orchids. But anyway, my grandmother would look delighted and bring the flowers in as if they were long-lost friends or a baby left on her *umbral*, and

I could imagine her cutting the stems like this, slantwise, I could picture my offerings in the kitchen or the room where they sat all day with my grandfather, brooding about their daughter, where I would never ever *nunca jamás* be invited in."

"And your aunts and uncles?"

"Yeah, what about the rest of the family, miss?"

"The same thing," she says. "They all loved the flowers I brought them early, so early, before they could get up and catch who was bringing the gifts. Until one day, my grandmother looked up and saw me— it was raining that day, raining like it can only rain back there, the rains here in Philly are like a cat's piss compared to those rains, if you'll pardon the expression...."

"We've heard worse, miss."

"Much worse."

"...well, my grandmother saw me through the downpour hiding behind the mountain of that tree, peeping out at her," she says, "and I thought now she knows it's me, now she's going to throw the flowers out, trample them, curse them, flood me with words worse than the rain. But she didn't. She pretended she hadn't seen me and went back into the house with the flowers, and I knew it was alright, we'd never talk, I've never touched her hand or exchanged a word with her to this day, but that the flowers were there as my *embajadores*, you know, representing me. And the folks of Catalina, who weren't as harsh with us as my mother's family, though they had reason to resent our presence, the neighbors in Catalina would call me *la niña de las flores*, just like your father, they would say, shaking their heads, at times *iracundos*, at times just sad. And I couldn't understand what they meant. Was it good or was it bad that I was just like my father? I had never seen him."

"Never seen your father?"

"Not even in a photo," she says. "All I knew was that he had left Catalina in the dark, the very night my mother was giving birth to me, he had escaped our village before somebody killed him."

"Somebody wanted to kill him?"

"That's what I'd heard," she says. "And that he was waiting for us in the States, I also knew that, knew that one day we'd join him. But I never supposed it would be a place where there were no onions to eat from the fields or flowers to gather just like that, and that's when I got into trouble. Always the flowers, my mother said when they sent me home that day from school, the second day I had gone there. And my parents had to come to school the next day to discuss my suspension, and the strange thing was that my mother was more angry with my father than with me. It's fate, she said. It's the curse of the flowers, is what she said. Your father's fault."

"How could it be your father's fault if you'd been the one to steal those flowers, hundreds of them, the previous afternoon, if I'm not mistaken? Unless your father—?"

"Borrowed them," she says. "I borrowed them from those shops, a dozen different shops—"

"So you knew it was wrong, you made sure you wouldn't be caught."

"I told you you wouldn't understand," she says. "Look—this is something I always did back there, even after we left Catalina, when we moved. I had no more family to leave my flowers with, but I still kept on gathering flowers at dawn so I could arrive early at school and leave one on each desk, for each boy and girl and for each teacher, and again they called me *la niña de las flores*, even though they had no way of knowing that they were repeating what the people in Catalina used to call me. So I wanted to do the same thing here in Philadelphia, but I only managed to do it once, because my teacher asked me that morning where I'd got all the flowers from and how I'd paid for them and things like that. I could hardly speak any English at that point, but I could understand the teacher wasn't happy with me, but luckily Evangelina, she translated for me, she was in the desk next to mine, so lovely with the flower I'd given her peeking out of her hair."

"Did she have a flower in her hair when she died?"

"What do you mean?" she says.

"A flower, my friend here would like to know if when you found her she had a flower in her hair?"

"A flower?" she says. "Not that I remember. And I'd spent the afternoon before she—before she killed herself, I'd spent it with her. First she went to the hairdresser so she'd be pretty when I found her."

"She knew it would be you, miss."

"I think she knew," she says. "She'd put on her blue dress, the one I'd bought for her, so I'm sure. We found her there, lying very peacefully on her bed, on top of the covers, so as not to ruffle them. That's the sort of person Evangelina was."

"And you never suspected she would…"

"Not at all," she says. "Evangelina was angry, of course, because they'd closed the factory, in spite of all the experts and all the questions and all the promises, and it was the high-tech one and we all thought they'd shut ours down—you know, where I work as a nurse—because it was so much older. But you know, my mother and my brother also lost their jobs there and they didn't do anything like what Evangelina did."

"Your brother seems to have got into debt, miss."

"Gambling debts, miss, it seems."

"Nobody's perfect," she says. "Not him, not anybody. Certainly not me. I failed Evangelina, I should have seen what she—I'd even given her one of my famous massages the night before and my fingers didn't alert me to what she was planning, not at all. 'How do I look, Flower Girl?' she asked—that's what she called me, what everybody calls me. And I told her she looked like a million dollars. 'A million dollars,' she said. 'Good.' And then she kissed me good-bye and went home and wrote a letter to her mother in Puerto Rico and killed herself that very night. With pills she stole from her factory."

"You didn't give her those pills, did you, miss?"

"Because as a nurse you certainly had access to that sort of pills. We're not accusing you of anything, but we do need to know if…"

"Why would I give her those pills?" she says. "She was my best friend."

"That's the sort of thing we do for best friends, miss. We want to help them, right?"

"I would never do that," she says.

"You would never commit suicide, miss, is that what you mean? Because I think you've had some trouble with that sort of thing your-self, in the past, if we're not mistaken."

"Evangelina was desperate," she says. "She did what people do when they're desperate. We spend life dancing right on the edge and we dance as if there were no cliff nearby, even though some part of you knows you're taking an awfully big risk, that if one more bad thing hap-pens to you, you'll lose your footing, you'll slip and fall over that edge. Just one prayer that nobody answers will do it. One misstep. In her case that interview did it, at least that's what I think. If they'd fired her with-out asking her all those questions, I think she'd have managed just fine. But they humiliated her and that did her in."

"Did you know that Evangelina was scared, that she thought she was being watched by someone?"

"The police told me about that," she says, "yes."

"And you still think there is nothing suspicious about your friend's death?"

"Look," she says, "Evangelina was depressed, the door was locked from the inside and—besides, who would want to kill her? I mean, what sort of life is that, always looking over your shoulder to see if something terrible's going to happen. Look, let me tell you. I also feel at times that somebody's following me. Lots of women feel that."

"You know who it is, miss?"

"Have you talked it over, say, with your boyfriend?"

"With Johnny?" she says. "Of course not. I don't know who it is, don't care for that matter. How could I possibly know? Or Johnny? Why should anybody be interested in me?"

"So you don't feel you're in danger, miss?"

"In danger?" she says. "What do you mean?"

"In danger, miss."

"What my friend here means, have you felt that something might happen to you just like it happened to Evangelina?"

"Danger?" she says. "Why should I feel I'm in danger? Who would want to do anything to me? Why would I interest anybody enough to take the trouble?"

"We don't know, miss. We thought maybe you had the answer to that question."

SECOND PART

My soul was lost to God until that moment,
and wholly given over to avarice;
such was my sin, such is my punishment.

—DANTE, PURGATORIO, CANTO XIX, 115-117

FOUR

   nd it was then, sir, that I decid-
...**A** ed to come in. I'd been, of
course, monitoring the whole affair on
my portable video, attending to
Blake from the next room, waiting
for his face to show that he had
completed the first stage of
his enlightenment. I heard him
begin to confess, repent, tell Roxanna how he would make up for it, ready
to face charges.... Things had gone far
enough. It was time to congratulate him,
reveal myself, so to speak.

    "Congratulations," I said, stepping into the bed-
room.

    He'd dragged Roxanna to the bed, wrapped her in
blankets, was tending to her. He looked up, startled. Like a
mad man. It always happens. Patients are not, as you know, sir,
very original. They always react in the same way. As if they were, in

effect, lunatics.

"Congratulations, Mr. Blake," I repeated, emphasizing the *mister*, for the first time in a month not calling him just plain Blake. "Your therapy has been successful. You are cured. You need no longer entertain qualms about your morality, I take it."

He attacked me viciously, bitterly. What sense did it have to be cured, as I put it, and which he very much doubted, what sense if the price was the suffering of these people, the death of that innocent man, this poor suicide's life ruined? He'd see me in jail, even if it meant that he would also be prosecuted, we should all pay for this terrible crime.

I smiled at that, sir. His very words were proof, I said, that he was indeed cured. Really sane. "You care more about them," I said, "than you do about yourself." I explained to him that other patients had not fared so honorably, as you are aware, sir. They have surrendered to the inner demons tormenting them rather than grappling with them. They have watched the woman of their dreams—or the man—die, commit suicide, be raped, be tortured, and haven't crossed over to the other side to save them, haven't risked losing everything, haven't confessed. They just stalled, idled there in utter fascination, clicked for a close-up of the dying lips, watched the heart stop beating, the scream of pain. They were also cured. The therapy always works, I told Blake, because its goal is for the client to understand who he really is and act accordingly. "And what you've discovered," I said to him, "is that you may have done many improper things but that in spite of them, you are a good man. You have had your cake, Mr. Blake, and now you can eat it too."

"Cake? What the fuck are you talking about? Improper things?" He was beginning to rant, wasn't taking this revelation as well as his Rorschach had foretold. "Improper? She could have died. Like Johnny."

I said nothing. Waited. Preferred for him to experience the breakthrough, approach illumination by himself. I smiled a bit more to help him on his way. Nothing. So I nudged him along with an additional observation:

"You're a businessman, Mr. Blake. How much do you think it would cost us to have somebody really die? Think of it in purely cost-effective terms. Or in terms of capital risk. Would you invest in that sort of hedge fund, futures scheme, a country that could default that easily?"

I could see him thinking furiously, sir. I could see it dawning on him, everything falling into place.

"Aren't there less expensive ways of obtaining the desired effect? Aren't there?"

I gave him time.

"She's…" he started to say and then stopped.

"She's…" I coaxed him on.

"She's—she's… an actress." He stumbled over the words, stuttered them, sir. Didn't stammer the next ones: "My God," he said to her, went up to her there on the bed all covered with false vomit and spit, cradled in those blankets. "You're an actress. They—all of them. They've all been actors, they've all been—"

"Congratulations, again, one more time," I said to him. It's a moment, I'm sure you remember, when the patients' egos need to be massaged a bit, sir, when we have to build up their battered self-confidence. "You're not only ethical, Mr. Blake. You're also an extremely perceptive person. Most of our clients, even the few who do have the guts and the decency to risk crossing over to the other side, don't realize until we tell them that it's all been an extraordinary mise-en-scène just for them. Though the quality of the performances often depends on the quality of the script—and yours, Mr. Blake, was superb. You should have been a Hollywood producer."

I waved my hand, you know the gesture, sir, and the whole cast of characters trooped into the bedroom. First of all, Johnny, grinning. Maybe he was grinning because he got a full month's salary and only had to act out twenty-five minutes of seduction and foreplay and had spent the rest of the time on call, in case Blake suddenly demanded his return. And Sonia, who's really the best of them all, we're going to have to give her a raise or maybe even make her a partner, a junior partner, at any rate. Indispensable. And then in came Bud, who's had the time of his life, though he does ham it up a bit and our scene director has been try-ing to tone down some of his improvisations in rehearsal. But our Bud did make himself thoroughly obnoxious, did provoke Blake into lashing out, going over the deep end. So he'll get his bonus like they all will. And Fred and Jason and Silvia and Ned and all the extras as well, Ivan and Big Benjy and the policemen and the lighting designer and our prop man and the make-up artist and… well, there were enough of us crowded into that bedroom to shoot a movie which is more or less what we'd been doing, except that the camera consisted of Blake's eyes. And Roxanna, taking a bow now—what a bravura performance, sir.

We all began to clap and then Graham Blake joined in, smiling. He'd been had, conned for his own good, to prove his own good, and he was grateful. Though you'll be pleased to note, sir, in this videotape I'm leaving you, that our patient is trying, as we expected, to hide something dark inside and behind his eyes, behind his applause.

We all trudged over to our control room, where Sandra had pre-pared a banquet for us, both celebration and going-away party.

Blake was very noble. Gave everyone a hug. A specially long embrace to Roxanna. Though with a hint of—what should I call it?—tentativeness. She must have noticied that slight hesitation, timidity. "No hard feelings?" she asked. And he answered, "Of course not." But when he turned to thank me, take me in his arms, as he came toward me, I could see that he was wondering whether, as part of my duties, I also got to try out the merchandise. I could see he was thinking it, I knew he would ask me that question later on when we were by our-selves. But his crassness, when he finally popped it, surprised me, the fact that he no longer felt he needed to make any effort whatsoever to tame his tongue, hide his envy.

"Do you get to screw her? Roxanna? Or whatever her real name is. Is that also part of the deal, Tolgate, that you get to try out the mer-chandise before putting it on exhibition?"

I answered then, later on, I mean, in our follow-up session in Hous-ton, I answered as I usually do that it was none of his business, but implied that this sort of behavior would conflict with my personal ethics. He seemed to understand my point of view that high-energy intensive therapies can only be successful if the man in charge is above reproach. While it is happening, after all, I am aware, even if he isn't, that nobody is getting hurt or abused, nobody is using their domination to exact pleasure or power from others. Which is the way he would be, exercising utmost responsibility, when he got back to real life.

"You're going to have a sensational comeback, Mr. Blake. You've worked out your obsessions and found out that they do not influence your final moral decisions. You've come to terms with the difficult choices your job requires. Maybe you'll have to administer some pain. But it will all be done with the best interests of everyone in mind. You have proved to yourself that in an emergency, when things get nasty and you have to inflict some inevitable pain, you can trust that you will look out for the greater good, everyone's best interests."

You want to know how he took that?

My guess is extremely well. He believed me, let's say. For now.

One more interesting development.

Before that final session of ours ended, just after he had declared his total satisfaction, clearing the way for the rest of the three million dollars to be taken out of escrow and transferred into our account, he asked me:

"How did you know about my mother?"

"Your mother?"

He explained haltingly, taking his time, as if he were just recognizing the depth of the experience, plumbing it right then and there for hidden meanings. Apparently he accessed, at the culminating moment of the treatment, when Roxanna had bathed him with that look of approval and adoration that has become her trademark, he had stumbled upon a memory of his own mother when she had been dying. He paused, perhaps waiting for me to intervene, maybe merely struggling to put into words his emotional turbulence.

"I can't thank you enough for having cured me," he said. "I

thought she committed suicide. My mother. All these years, I've believed she killed herself. And that I sat by her side and watched her do it and did nothing to stop her. It's what I told myself. Nobody else. Just myself. And hardly even myself, hardly dared to tell myself. It would surface from time to time, the guilt, the…"

Again, he paused. This time I helped him out.

"And the therapy helped you to realize…"

"That it was a false memory. Seeing Roxanna really killing herself—well, it seemed real to me—made me perceive that my mother hadn't died like that. In my mind I saw what… I remembered my mother dying peacefully. Thanks to the treatment, I now know that I wasn't to blame."

"You weren't to blame," I agreed. "You're right. You probably made up that traumatic memory of your mother committing suicide to compensate for surviving, to punish yourself for not having saved her. And kept on feeling guilty about that and then about other things, so many other things."

"What I don't understand," Blake said again, taking his time, "is how you knew about my mother, what I felt about her death. I mean, that's why you planned a suicide at the end, right? Roxanna told me that she had been looking forward to that final scene all month. Her tour de force, she said. So she knew, you knew, it was coming. Where my story would end up, no matter how I had scripted it before. Only—how did you know? That it was what I needed?"

I told him that most of our therapies finish with that sort of flourish, a dramatically staged suicide at the end or some other form of extreme violence that tests the patient. I told him that I don't believe much in Freudian theories and prefer my own Therapy Through Acting hypothesis, an almost necessary corollary of Tolgate's syndrome. In his case, it had been a lucky guess, a lucky coincidence.

I don't think he was convinced, sir. He sees me as almost omnipotent. A mind reader. Someone who can invade dreams. Which is not a bad thing for him to think, given what is still to come.

As for that voracious question you're asking with your eyes right now, sir—that question Graham Blake asked me point-blank about Roxanna and my connection to her—I didn't answer him then and I certainly am not going to answer you now.

I believe that I established the specific rules and limits of our relationship when you were good enough to bankroll this business, after you yourself were fortunate enough to go through our therapy, the inaugural launch, so to speak. You may recall that I promised you the profits would be substantial, and they have been. As to the future, with four million multimillonaires in this country alone and more pressure than ever on them to both rack up profits and at the same time appear more and more ethical, well, there should be a good number of mental breakdowns, and we expect healthy growth in revenue.

But it was clear at our first meeting—and we have pursued the matter on later occasions—that the unrestricted access to the confidential files, tapes, transcripts of the patients that has been granted to you, and which you have savored, if I might say so, quite exhaustively, does not extend into my own private life or, for that matter, to the intimate details of the existence of any of our staff and/or performers. I'm off limits, sir, and intend to remain so. That is, after all, what matters in life, it all comes down to this choice: are we to be the eye that watches the microbe or are we fated to become the microbe that is watched by some superior eye?

A choice our friend Graham Blake will soon face as his therapy enters its next phase.

I'll keep you informed, sir.

Enjoy the tapes. And please return them to me when you're done.

FIVE

I watch them because I can no longer
watch you, Roxanna, Roxanna not
mine, not even Roxanna. I know it's
crazy to be speaking to you like this
inside my head, but to whom else
can I pour out my secrets but
someone who doesn't exist,
who won't judge me, who started
me out on this path to... shall I call
it freedom, can I call what I am doing,
what is happening to me, freedom?

Have you thought of me ever again? Do
you think of Graham Blake now, at this very
moment when you're probably off somewhere playing the same role or a different one for another executive
as screwed up as I was, tempting him to confront himself,
am I in your thoughts as you are in mine as you drain him of
his bitter insomnia with your slow-motion waltz across a living

room, across his screen? Is it the same character? Or another one, from another country, with another family, but always you with your glide, that silent floating-flower walk of yours.

Or maybe that was only for me, a performance only to save me. I try to convince myself that you're not repeating those gestures for another man, hope they were conceived exclusively for Graham Blake, something nobody else will ever have access to. But then I think no, it's much better if that's how you really are, the image you presented to me of a cheerful, mysterious, magical Roxanna no more than a mirror of your true self rather than a performance. I hope that's who I'm directing these words to. You cured me, after all—aren't you curious to know what happened to your sole audience and solitary patient and faraway admirer? Don't tell me you don't ask Tolgate about me, aren't gladdened by his news that everybody around me thinks I'm fine.

And I am fine, I am. Except that those who surround and observe and congratulate me, they're also wrong, they haven't the slightest inkling of what I am really going through. Oh, I sleep well, and I've come back bursting with energy from my one-month vacation at what I tell people was a "fabulous spa," yes, and I've been able to launch the smartest campaign the company ever cooked up, "Downsizing with a Heart," that has won us accolades from the right and the left and the center, not to mention that all the tough decisions that had accumulated at my desk were dispatched without a tremble in my fingers or a headache in my temples. And just as significant, Natasha is overjoyed at this savage and tender lover whom you have sent her, yes, you sent her this gift, she's astonished, Natasha is, at how wise and restrained and considerate I now am and… and… what else? Maybe Tolgate has told you that I received the highest honor that can be conferred by the Global Marketers Association, the Best Boss in the World award for my "everlasting contribution to a new image of global companies as caring and compassionate and competitive." If I ever meet you again, I could show you clips of that evening a few nights ago when I spoke to one thousand guests at two thousand dollars a head, two million dollars for the starving kids of the Sudan, I'll tell you all about how they fêted me, celebrated my latest accomplishments. You couldn't be doing better, they said to me, slapping me on the back. And that's true. Everything's on the upswing for me. And then one of them added, The sanest man on this clean earth of ours. Yeah, a chorus of *yeahs* from the others: Wish we had your health, your energy. But they don't know. They don't know that I don't believe them, that I am watching them, I can't stop watching them. Insanely watching them all, my enemies who masquerade as my friends. Yes, insanely.

I don't want to feel like this. I don't like the Graham Blake who murmurs this to you in his mind. But I'm not going to kill him, not prepared to feign, as I have all these years, that he's not here, inside me, speaking to you.

I realized that I would have to coexist with him, with who I had become, the first night I was back, Roxanna not mine. Natasha had fallen asleep, exhausted from our athletic bout in bed, and I lay by her side holding her hand, stroking her blond hair, then sat up in bed, examined her, so near and so far from me. Those dreams I would never see myself. That body I could never entirely possess. So what else is new?

This is new, Roxanna, who will not be mine, who I once thought might be mine: I stood up and went to my study. I didn't even know what I was trying to find until I opened a drawer and took it out, there where I know Hector keeps it, there it was, the camcorder, and that was it, what I craved. I went back to our bedroom, to the threshold, out of Natasha's immediate line of sight in case she awoke, and fixed the camera on her. For a while I didn't press the record button, merely zoomed in and out as if I were fucking her with the lens, cruised along her body with the stealth you had taught me with your lackadaisical movements, took my time and then and only then pressed the button and logged her into celluloid memory, bagged her like a slumbering wild animal. And then, and only then, when an hour had passed, did I take the video to the next room and slipped it into the home video system and there, up on the screen here in my Houston penthouse as large as the one-way mirror that separated me from your fake bathroom, I rewound and watched Natasha sleeping, breathing the night in the way you had back there in Philadelphia, breathing it out, returned to the wonder of that adventure when I could do whatever I wanted to you, realizing oh so slowly that I could also do now whatever I wanted to Natasha. If I killed her, had her killed, nobody would ever know. I have the power, I have the money, I have the imagination, I can conceive plots, concoct scenarios in my head that will never be carried out, but that could, that could. That could if I had the desire to hurt anybody. Not that I would think of it. Those eyes of yours looked into the deepest part of me and that was true, that had to be true. It could not have been acting: it was you probing into me, I saw myself in those maternal eyes, you saw me and returned me to myself. "Whatever you do, it's for the best," you said to me. "Finally, you were willing to take the blame for the disaster you had created," those eyes of yours were saying. "Only a good man would have done that." I think you were right, Roxanna, when your eyes said that.

So, what's wrong with me? What's wrong is that if I want to sleep, if I want to rest… there's a price to pay, there's a price for everything, my Roxanna who is not even called Roxanna. I am forced to secretly film the secret world that threatens me. That's what my body asks of my hands, that's the final outcome of our month together. You cured me of any doubts about my own morality—but now I fill the time that I used to waste worrying and obsessing, in another sort of activity. Now I spend the day devouring images or thinking about how I can witness what people near me do, everything they do.

I slept well that first night. Not much, but deeply. And awoke early the very next day, before Natasha, and it was absolutely clear to me what I needed to do if I was to have peace of mind: Before breakfast I had called Sweet Spies Incorporated, and agreed on a price to wire my apartment with hidden cameras. I then made sure to send Hector at noon to deliver some gifts to my kids on the other side of town, gave the maid the day off, rushed back from the office at midday to supervise the service being installed in each room. Just like when I was with

you, Roxanna, back in Philadelphia. Except that now I'm in real control, the only one to whom I whisper this plot a woman who doesn't
exist and can't hear me. There's nobody here but myself manipulating
the buttons and switches in my private bathroom where nobody enters,
not even Hector. So I can watch Natasha at my leisure, watch the ser-
vants, watch the kids when they come to visit. Watch myself.

I tried one night not to look at my videos, I tried, Roxanna. And
the headaches came slithering back into my skull, and the reptile
thoughts in my mind that would not let me rest, and the irritation. The
desire to smash faces, again, again. And then a quick look, a quick fix:
like a drug.

Not only in my apartment: everywhere. I have hired detectives to
film, register, record. Follow Jessica around. Or my son at the playground. Then I step into the picture. That night Graham Blake
watches Graham Blake with his son at the playground. My best
friend, Sam Halneck. The man who guided me to the Corporate Life
Therapy Institute. I've taped his most intimate moments with his
wife, catfights they've had, insults back and forth smearing their sexless nights. I know things about them they have forgotten.

Memory, said Dr. Tolgate, is the art of forgetting. Not for me, not
for my camera, not for my satellites. Because I can watch my friends
and partners playing at being themselves over and over, till I know them
by heart, zeroing in on the moment that reveals it all, exposes the hidden guts of the experience that they have already erased in order to
keep living. And do you know what I do then, Roxanna? Then I go to
dinner with them, and use that knowledge to manipulate both Sam
and Miriam, steer the conversation to the one subject they'd rather
avoid and watch them squirm. They're in my hands. I've stolen their
life. But not for long: I give it back to them, let them off the hook, back
off and save them from embarassment. They end up feeling indebted
to me. Then I can go home and click and switch and watch how I
watched them squirm. And wake up the next morning after a refresh-
ing sleep, ready to go, full of vim, on top of the world. And drive off to

the office. Where I've also installed a video security system. Every shift and twirl and evasion of every employee, at my fingertips. I've had snoops prowl the halls of my factories and buildings making believe they are reporters gathering information for their shows. I've got hundreds of tapes. Thousands. More than I'll ever be able to view. Every e-mail searched for key words, tracked, underscored.

I started this vast spying project for health reasons. Or so I told myself at the beginning: it's just a transitory continuation of my therapy, I murmured to the Graham Blake, the old one, who would never have done anything like this to the people he loves and works with. The new Graham Blake, the Best Boss in the World, he has a different philosophy: As long as you don't hurt anybody permanently, why should it matter what you do, how you enjoy yourself. A good man can ultimately do no harm. Learned from you and Dr. Tolgate. That I shouldn't deny myself the pleasure of that moment when I press the play button, yanked back to the thrill of seeing you through the glass partition, through the eye of the camera.

Of course, you also schooled me in a new tempo of life, a painstaking approach which allows things to surface without haste. The only way to really discover anything: Wait for it, that's what you would say. So it's not surprising it took me a while to discover that my obsession was rooted in something more essential, beyond the first rush of pleasure, a foreboding that a zone of me did not want to release until I was ready to face it: I'm taping the people around me because it's the only way to survive. Roxanna, you'd understand. You, who lived for one month with a camera up your pretty ass, down your cleavage, inside your shower. That's what they want to do with me. I'm sure. Just like something was murmuring to me that you weren't quite real, you couldn't be real—that same something is warning me.

They're out to get me.

They haven't made their move yet. I had my offices combed, had my apartment examined. They must be waiting for me to let my guard down, lulled into confidence, langour, laxness. Then they'll install their cameras. Try to capture me. Probe me the way I used to probe you.

Who are they?

That's what I am going to find out. Because they don't know that I'm a step ahead, watching them. They don't know that I have my favorite moments. The moments I have repeated over and over until I've been able to squeeze from them the secrets that are being concealed from me.

Why were they all so anxious to send me off to the Corporate Life Therapy Clinic? What happened in that month while I was gone, curing myself with you and your family, Roxanna?

Here are the moments that betray their true intentions:

First moment. I'm at the Hilton, receiving the Best Boss in the World Award. Look at me work the crowd, promise one guy that we'll do business, postponing shady deals with the next member of the club, giving him a maybe, a call-me-later, and always espousing my mantra that competition and compassion are not incompatible, are complementary at the global level. There's Jessica—my wife and partner, former wife, present partner, should I say—coming up to give me a kiss. Hasn't given me a kiss in a long time. A mistake, that kiss. Rouge with the smell of apples. And a whiff of another perfume, musk oak, who knows, along with the apples.

"When are we going to get together, you and me?"

As if we don't meet every day at work, didn't have dinner with each other last week, aren't going to picnic with the kids this Sunday.

"When are we going to get together?"

She means it. Wants to mean it. But I've been trained, you've trained me, Roxanna who was not even then Roxanna, who fooled me then but would not fool me now—just as Jessica can't. She's acting. She's pretending. My ex. Disguised, masked, lip-synching. Pretending she's drunk so I will buy her sincerity, so she can deny her words tomorrow in case she needs to.

"I miss you." Said so low that even I can hardly hear it. Those red-ripe lips with the scent of apple.

I'm rescued by Natasha—who's also playing some sort of game, though I think she's not in their pay. I've examined the tapes. What is she hiding? Is she in debt? Wants the money? Or am I being unfair? Am I in the throes, as Snow Princess Sonia would have alleged, of a bad sequel? Maybe. Natasha probably loves me as much as I love her. Did I tell you that I loved her, or at least liked her? She's a sport. When you've watched someone sleeping for hours, you can tell. You end up knowing. And I am indebted to her for extricating me from the clutches of that vixen Jessica. If my former wife were not the primary partner in this business, I would…

We get into our limo. Who do you think is there?

Look at the video, let me flick it on.

That's Hank Granger. Maybe you know Hank Granger? As a client, maybe? As something else? Did you ever look at him as you looked at me? Granger who sits in my limo as if he owns it. As if he will own it soon. Get a life, Granger. Haven't I told you I'm not selling?

"You're going to ruin the business," Granger whispers to me. What matters is that he comes obscenely close, his breath creeps up to my mouth. "You've ordered a study on how to upgrade that rickety factory in Philadelphia. Deny it."

I'm not going to deny anything. I'm not even listening to his tiresome comments—of course I want that factory upgraded. It's the one where you work, Roxanna. The one you purported to work at. Feigned you were going to in the morning, feigned you were praying for its workers in the evening, feigned you were cleansing yourself of its grime in the nights. My dad's factory. I'm going to save it because it belongs to my dad and to you and to me, belongs to your nonexistent families and those families that do exist and need its beating pulse, need to be producing those cereals and teas and ointments for their health, the health of America, my health. Saved because it's my past, our common heritage, I can still remember walking down its corridors and someone holds my hand and I look up and it's my mother, and I'm not going to strip that place of its memories and turn it into a condominium or a mall and chockfill it with strangers.

That's not what I thought then as a child. It's what I think now as I review the tape, hurl insults at Granger in the late night hours while Natasha sleeps in our bed, insatiable sweet Natasha, a better fuck than you'd have been, Roxanna, but not as intriguing, not such a good actress, not as slow on her feet, not able to pray. Were you praying for me, Roxanna? Did your prayers cure me? Not even the pope could have cured me with his prayers. And the pope doesn't have such a cute ass. But that's not what I thought when Granger approached me with his puffy exhalation. I didn't think anything. I just smelled him. On his lips the faintest trace of apple musky oil: the intimation and hint of Jessica on his tongue. When did he kiss her? When did she come close enough to his mouth, stream words into his mouth instead of his ears, when was that? Did they fuck before she showed up at the Best Boss in the World ceremony? Before he dropped into my limo to wait for me because he's so disreputable they wouldn't have let him into the ballroom at the Hilton? Or am I making all this up, is it the vestige of Jessica swirling in my nostrils that pervades everything, infecting even my future with her memory? Am I paranoid? Is that what my month with you and Tolgate, that ménage à trois, did to me?

"You're bleeding the company to death. It makes no business sense." Granger blows the words my way, as if he were smoking Jessica in my direction. "Sell the company to me now, your share. I'll triple your stock options and keep you on as vice president. Or do you want to wait for bankruptcy? When your sentimental Godzilla money pit drags you down?"

I don't say a word. Something, something inside—is it you, Roxanna, whispering your protection?—tells me to wait one more instant, Granger is about to give me the clue I have been searching for, what I'll need in the days to come to fend him off, unmask him.

And he gives it to me, gives it to me even if he doesn't know what he's doing.

"Pathetic," says Granger. "You know what you are? Like one of those victims of King Kong—blind and stupid and about to be crushed. Crushed by a sentimental Godzilla money pit."

I kicked him out of the limo, Roxanna. I mean literally put my foot on his ass and gave him a shove, sent him sprawling onto the sidewalk. You'd have been proud of me—you or at least the working-class woman you made believe you were. The sham woman who thought we had to help others if we were to help ourselves. The woman Tolgate constructed and scripted because it was the woman I needed to have faith in. Or maybe you are her, maybe you already knew Spanish, the real thing all along, and that's why Tolgate chose you for the part.

But I am digressing from our little tour through my favorite videos. Another moment of truth. The next scene brought forth as evidence is in the ladies' lavatory, Clean Earth headquarters, city of Houston. There they are, a group of secretaries, peeing, powdering, laughing. It's the gossip I adore. Not only who's screwing who, though I don't mind finding out that my chief operations officer has got a dick the size of a baby chick's beak and can hardly get it up. That Jessica Owen's got a mystery suitor and nobody can track down his identity. Even more interesting: They're worried about the future of the Company. Word is out that the boss is upgrading the Philadelphia plant when he should be getting rid of it. Word is out that the Company is in trouble and will be merged, acquired, taken over by somebody they don't approve of. Somebody who wants to get his sleazy hands on our incredible breakthrough in alternative food technology that is about to be approved by the FDA: a dietary pill that makes you lose weight the more you eat, the more you guzzle and gobble. In fact that's what I've called it for now, the Gobbler, though I'm not sure if that name will make the final cut.

Not that I have the time now to wonder about alternatives. Something more important is on my mind. I recognize what they're doing, think I do. You guided me, Roxanna, taught me well, indicated how to tell what's real, what's simulated: and their conversation seems rehearsed to me. They're not as good as you are at this. That line, "Do you think he'll keep on trying to save that stupid plant?" and then the response like a red stoplight in the wet night: "More than stupid. It's a sentimental Godzilla money pit." Granger's words. Granger scripting them? Granger knowing that I'm taping these women and will hear them, fear that things are spinning out of control? Or he doesn't know the specifics of my spying and it doesn't matter because those words he planted—*sentimental, Godzilla, money pit, stupid, stupid*—will swarm out into the corridors and cubbyholes and online chatroom of Clean Earth anyway, will reach my ears, other ears: encirclement strategy. Though a tiny voice of reason inside me acts as a reminder that maybe it's the other way around and Granger picked those words up from women like these, maybe they're in the air, mouth-to-mouthing in the air.

Third and last moment I like to browse, scrutinize: dinner at Sam Halneck's. Late cognac and cigars on Sam's terrace overlooking the city. I've already played every trick in the trade on him, am going easy tonight, thanking him for having steered me to Tolgate's embrace, to your guiding dance and light, Roxanna. Look at him. Long draw on the cigar. "Did me a world of good too," Sam says, sighing. "Wish they'd take women. I'd send Miriam there in a jiffy. Would really cool her out. Her PMS is driving me off the wall, brother, I'll tell you." But now is what matters, what comes now: "You know why they say women aren't allowed? You know why? Because he hates women."

"Tolgate?" I ask Sam, surprised. Not pretending. Really surprised. Because Tolgate likes the gentler sex, the way in which he drove up and down your thighs with his eyes, Roxanna—nobody can tell me the good doctor isn't one hot male horde of hormones.

"No," Sam says, leaning forward. No scent of apples on his lips. He hasn't been fucking my former wife. Has enough trouble just fucking his own, if we are to believe what our eyes see when we flick on his bedroom with my remote control and he falls asleep before he can service poor Miriam, no wonder she's such a resentful bitch. "No," Sam repeats. "The big, big boss. The owner. The guy who's bankrolling the Corporate Therapy Life Institute."

"Who?" I ask.

"You're not going to like this."

"I already don't."

"A friend of mine swears it's Granger. Doesn't seem likely. I can't see Granger investing in anything that would assuage the pain of his fellow humans. But then, it's only a rumor. Though it would explain why no women are admitted to—"

"And you knew about this when you recommended that I—"

He says do I think he's crazy. Of course not. He'd never have handed me over to an institute owned by my main rival, that unscrupulous bastard. And Sam's telling the truth as far as I can tell. Unless he's a better actor than even you are, than my cold Sonia was. Did she fake those orgasms as well? To make me think she was falling for me so she could set me up? Or did her instructions allow her to luxuriate in herself, get her kicks even while she's toying with a client? Would your instructions have allowed you, Roxanna, to have slipped into my bed if I had found a way to bring you over? Or was I always out of bounds? And who determined those instructions finally? Who was the shadow behind the shadow of Tolgate? Was it really Granger? Has all this been organized to nail me, manipulate me into carrying out the plans he's brewed up with Jessica, is this only the first stage of a conspiracy that has many cameras and many control rooms and many one-way mirrors, somebody watching me from the other side of the wall as I surf these videos attempting to ferret out the details, like nails in a coffin that have to be jimmied loose, is there a ruthless Graham Blake out there waiting for the moment to destroy me?

You hold the answer, Roxanna. If I were able to see you again, watch that performance of yours… I've become adept at this. I remember that moment when Tolgate introduced us, so to speak, that moment when you began to delude me and I began to believe what my eyes were seeing: Your little therapy, he said, and that flicker of recognition on your face, or was it fear? Was it fear? More than just knowing that somebody was on the other side watching. Fear of something else. If I could access you, fondle that moment, weed out what was really happening. Compare it to our last moment together, the one image of you that was automatically taped by the cameras but that I never got to see through the screen and repeat over and over because I had walked into the image, I was being watched rather than watching. It is the moment when your secret is being revealed, when Tolgate steps into the room where I am acting out my role as savior.

What would your eyes tell me if, in retrospect, knowing what I now know, I could see them again on a screen? Would they warn me to be wary, would I deduce that you are under a threat? Is there a hint of fear and does it belong exclusively to the false woman called Roxanna, a simulation of fear, or is it the real you who is scared, scared for me and not for herself, is it the actress who, underneath her performance, is aware that she has participated in merely one more scene in a greater drama that has yet to entirely unfold? Aware that somebody was going to go on scripting my life, had been scripting it for several years now? Was there a final flash of pity flaring gently in you, Roxanna, saying poor man, poor Graham, because you knew that this was just beginning?

If I could access you, that final moment when you changed from Roxanna the victim into somebody else, the triumphant woman who reveals she's been fooling me all this time, if I could only…

I tried. Asked Tolgate on the most recent of my monthly follow-through sessions. Yesterday in fact. Told him I was fine. Not a word about these attacks of voyeurism, my hankering for a woman who doesn't exist except in Tolgate's head and my head, you are there, Roxanna who is not there, suspended midway between the doctor and myself, joining him and me through your invisible body that hangs in the adulterous air between us.

Affecting nonchalance, I wonder if he could get me a copy of one of the tapes. The last one, I say to him. The one where I save Roxanna, where she saves me, where I begin to confess to her. And maybe the first one as well, when she walks into my life.

"Why do you want it?"

"I'm a sentimental bastard."

Not a good reason, but that "s" word was slushing around in me, the *sentimental* word, Granger had infected me with it. Tolgate retorts with his own "s" word: security. No can do. For security reasons. Everything's been shredded, all evidence. If it got out, if proof circulated of the clinic's methods, there would be no more treatment, no more business. "Like me asking you for the formula of your special herb balms, your famous floral essences," he said. "The ones that come out of that Phildelphia factory. The one you swore you wouldn't shut down." He paused, Roxanna. "Which brings me to a question I've been meaning to ask you. When Clean Earth does shut that old factory down, how do you think you'll deal with it? I mean, given that it was handed to you by your father, entrusted to you and all that."

"And when is this supposed to happen?"

"Why, this month."

I lost my temper, Roxanna. I shouldn't have. You'd scold me. You'd tell me that I should only lose my temper when I'm in command, when I'm not playing into somebody's hands. But it does seem as if everywhere I go each last person has an opinion about that old industrial plant that I've sworn to defend.

I told him it was a preposterous lie. "There is no way I'm going to throw Roxanna into the street," I spat out at Tolgate. That's what I said to him, I swear I said that to him.

"She doesn't exist, Graham," Doctor Tolgate admonished me gently. "You can't throw her into the street."

"Others. People like her is what I meant. Throw them out into the street."

"What you're about to do," Tolgate insisted. "Many others. This magazine says those are your plans."

He shows me a left-wing rag, sensationalistic, full of intellectual gobbledygook about globalization and human rights and NAFTA and uprooting and downsizing and the World Trade Organization—and there it is, an item on the imminent shut-down of the Clean Earth factory, the original one. To be transferred to Monterrey, Mexico. Or maybe Bangkok. Or Nairobi? It would have already happened, according to the magazine, if it weren't for the sentimental partner, Jessica Owen. The former wife of CEO Graham Blake, the woman who is the brains behind Clean Earth, has refused to bow to pressure to close it, says that there are still wonderful products coming from that place and she, for one, takes the company's motto seriously, "Downsizing with a Heart," and that's a hell of a big heart we're talking about.

The next day I confronted Jessica, you can believe I did. I accused her outright of sabotaging my plans to keep my dad's factory open.

"Sabotage? Those are big words. I've lost whole days away from the lab defending your idiotic decision to keep that factory open."

"Sabotage. You want proof? I asked for an upgrade-study three months ago."

"When you came back from your so-called vacation."

"Three months ago, and it's still not ready, there's still no solution."

Jessica looks at me with those eyes I have seen closed in pleasure, opened in pleasure, those eyes that I would gladly burn with a stick, scratch out, scratch out the memory of the pleasure she gave me, I gave her. She sees what I am thinking, grows pale.

"Graham," she says, "what in heaven has gotten into you? The study you asked for isn't ready because you keep on sending it back when it states there is no good solution, that you should close the motherfucker money pit down. And it's going to get worse: We have information that a strike's being planned at your dear father's favorite factory. We'd better find a way out of this predicament before the bad PR hits the fan. Use the money to upgrade the five plants that can be saved. Concentrate on our newest breakthrough."

I want her to think I'm mollified, that maybe I'm willing to play along.

"Give me some time," I say to her. "It's not easy. My dad, you know. My mom."

And she also relaxes, relents somewhat, gives me a quick peck on the lips. No scent of apple. No scent of Granger.

Am I going crazy, Roxanna? Am I as capricious and arbitrary as I am being made out to be? And is it true, are you planning a strike? You. I mean the workers at the factory you supposedly worked at. Are you planning anything? Ruining my plans to save you?

As soon as Jessica goes off to her lab and her breakthrough invention—maybe the Gobbler is not such a good name, maybe it's too infantile, selfish. How about Paradise Pills? Nirvana Nutrients?—I call my staff in, wave Tolgate's article at them, tell them that if there are any further leaks to the press about this matter, I will, for the first time in my life, be forced to fire an employee willingly and with gusto. Gusto. That Spanish word. Are you singing in Spanish now, Roxanna, stepping out of your shower while Tolgate blocks the view of some rival of mine, one of the men who pounded me on the back at my awards dinner?

Where are you?

And then I sit down at my desk and begin to go through recent tapes I have ordered from Paul St. Martin, the manager of my Philadelphia plant. Surfing to find signs of what is happening there, what's being hidden from me. Remembering how my father used to take me down those corridors, past those machines, taking a detour through the flower division and its dank smells of foreign lands. He knew each person name by name, son by daughter: Always remember, Graham, that they're the ones who make us rich, put food on our table. We risk our money for them. They risk their muscles and health and memories for us. Never forget that, son.

My mother's hand in my other hand.

I fast-forward to a part of the tape designated "cafeteria." The old cafeteria. My first peanut butter and jelly sandwich. Because Mom never wanted me to have anything that vulgar, that American. There I am, at five years old, here I am on this screen scrawling inside my head.

Not on any tape. Pure and marvelous memory. The unadulterated past. Betting the workers who were seated with me that I could get the old crone who worked at the cashier's register to give me another sandwich for free. Charming her out of another one by promising to cure her arthritis, massaging the back of her neck and hump while I winked at the men sitting there at the table, came back triumphant with my second sandwich. Without having paid for it. Already learning to sell something for nothing, Roxanna. Already learning my profession.

There it is, those tables, those dirty fluorescent low lights, those pictures of pastures my father put up to enliven the atmosphere. It should be upgraded also, modernized, made sleek—but I like it the way it is, run-down as it is, as if my past were waiting for me there, my first taste of peanut butter sandwiches with jelly waiting for me there. What's waiting for me is, in fact, a group of women workers. Coffee-break time. Not talking about any strike. Any takeover. Sex. Husbands. Children. The delayed shipment of jasmine flowers from India. Abortions. The latest twist in some soap opera. I'm about to fast-forward.

I'm about to fast-forward.

But now. But now. Now. Now one of the jabbering women calls across the cafeteria, calls somebody named Rose. Rose! she says. Over here, she says, hey, Flower Girl, motioning for that somebody to join them for some coffee. And Rose steps into the camera's range. Slowly, oh so slowly steps into the camera's range.

It's not you, Roxanna, it's not you at all. Not your hair, not your hips, no movie star quality to her: but she pauses as she glides by in her nurse's dress, Rose pauses and looks up, she looks straight at the hidden camera that is registering this for me, that registered it for me a few weeks ago. Rose stares into the lens and it is the same smile, the same look. I am back in my control room in that apartment in Philadelphia watching you arrive into my life. Rose is stockier, less pretty, wispy brown hair, darker skin, a less sulky sort of radiance, but she's smiling, she's smiling at some secret, she's as cheerful as you are, used to be. It's a coincidence, of course. It's one of those things that...

But I can't shake her, Roxanna, I can't shake the memory of that Rose in Philadelphia, the real nurse at the real factory.

It ruins my evening, it ruins the surprise Natasha's prepared for me. She's tried on the brunette wig I bought for her—fun and games, I said, and she played along—decked up in the dress I insisted that she put on today, a dead ringer, that blue dress, for one you wore the first night I saw you, Roxanna. Natasha, ready for love, coaxed into wetting my fingers with her mouth before she brings them to the button on her blouse, imitating without realizing it what you and Johnny were doing that night. Provoking me, you two back then, so I would put a stop to it, both of you stripping for me more than for each other. And now I am in the shot, now it is me and Natasha undressing each other for real while a different camera whirls and swirls, now it is me inside her, impatient in spite of what you had ingrained into my mind, Roxanna, not taking my time at all. Eager to be watching the video of this seduction, eager to be rewinding my own lovemaking. As soon as Natasha falls asleep, apparently satisfied, strangely spent by my inadequate thrusts, I'm out of there. I creep into my bathroom and rewind the tape and there we are, in the semidarkness we could almost be Roxanna and Johnny, you and your false Johnny, it could almost be you and me, Roxanna and Graham, as I tousle your black hair and slip that dress you wore that night from your shoulders, complete the blue lovemaking you never carried out with Johnny. Were never meant to carry out. Only doing it back then, you two, so I would stay for the month. I watch myself and the woman who could be you, I—

The door bursts open. It's Natasha. No wig. No dress. No prayer in her outstretched hand. She sees what I'm up to. I forgot to lock the door, forgot to keep an eye open for her. The possibility that she might not be asleep, might be faking it, faking everything, never crossed my mind.

She insults me. Not the words you would have used. You wouldn't have slapped me like she does. Natasha. Says I'm sick. Says she's tired of me and my games, my fun and games. Says she's leaving. Don't leave, Natasha, don't—

Slam goes the front door.

I could care less. I go back to the video. I said I could care less, but the truth is that the magic spell of her real body in the video brings her to me in all my loss, deriding my self-delusion. It's my loyal, patient, funster Natasha there, it's me forcing her to repeat the words that you said to Johnny, were in fact enunciating, Roxanna, for my benefit. Impossible to pretend I don't care that I've lost Natasha. You can't fuck a video, cuddle a video, a video can't speak back to you, challenge you as she did, fry my eggs. Eggs like I want them: almost burned to a crisp underneath, and the yolk still runny, creamy, on top. My Natasha. It's not true I couldn't care less. I really do like her, I really thought we could make something special together, Natasha and me.

In a rage I destroy every camera, all the video equipment, hammer the camcorder into a pulp, burn the tapes. And not one of those tapes contains even an intimation of you, Roxanna mine who is less and less mine as the hours go by, as the videos burn, as your memory fades and is replaced by Natasha's wig, the imitation blue dress I got for her.

It is the first night I cannot sleep since you looked into my eyes when I saved you, thought I was saving you on that bathroom floor. Since you convinced me that I had nothing to fear from myself.

I call Dr. Tolgate up, rouse him out of his own obviously untroubled sleep at three in the morning.

"This is Graham Blake."

"The answer is no," he says. Just like that. I haven't even asked him for anything and he says no already.

"No to what?"

"No, I already informed you that our clinic does not have a copy of the tape, any of the tapes you want. Neither the first one nor the last one. Isn't that why you called me?"

"How did you guess?"

"You're not the only patient I've treated, Mr. Blake. Typical aftereffect of what is called Tolgate's syndrome. Go back to sleep. Forget the tape. Reality is always infinitely more interesting."

I don't hang up. I have a question he's not expecting, I suppose he's not expecting it.

"How much do you get paid, Dr. Tolgate?"

"Enough to pay the bills."

"I could pay you more."

"I don't think so. They're very expensive bills, Mr. Blake."

"How much does he give you?"

"I don't know who you're talking about."

"Do you get a percentage of the companies he takes over when your patients go crazy? Is that the gimmick?"

"If you're trying to get me angry, Mr. Blake, you're not going to succeed. What you have to understand is that your reaction is—let me repeat this—absolutely normal. At this stage in the patient's therapy, the aggressive reflex invariably comes into play. Paranoia. Everybody's an actor, everybody's out to get you. Rest assured, it's only a passing phase."

And with that he hangs up on me. Leaving me to contemplate this empty penthouse for the next few hours. Trying to remember your face, Roxanna. Trying to remember Natasha's face. Without a tape to cradle me to sleep.

As if all this weren't bad enough, this morning Jessica comes by early. With a big breakfast basket. Making up for our little spat yesterday. Getting back into the mode of isn't-it-time-we-got-together-again?

"What in the hell happened here?" Jessica asks, inspecting the disarray of reels and tapes and pieces of surveillance equipment and camcorder parts strewn all over the living room. "I hate to meddle, Graham darling, but you need help, I hope you know that."

I don't answer her. I'm starving. I munch on a bagel, butter another one before I've wolfed the first one down, gulp down some freshly squeezed orange juice. It would make anybody hungry to ravage their own lives, their own illusions.

"At times I think you do stupid things just to spite me," Jessica says, in a good mood, trying to put a bizarre, almost droll, spin on the mess we're sitting in.

That finally gets a response from me. Dour, but a response. "You? Spite you? How do you always manage to claim the center spotlight in my life, even when, as in this case, you've got nothing, I mean, zilch, nothing, to do with any of this, Jessica. Believe me, you are not even remotely the reason I destroyed this equipment."

"It's just that you have this incredible knack," she insists, "of guessing my plans and then foiling them. It's exasperating precisely because it's unconscious. Last night you demolished every cassette machine in the apartment. Almost as if you knew that I was coming by this morning with a video that I wanted you to view."

I didn't know. What video is she talking about?

We see it on our way to Clean Earth headquarters. In the limo. With its cassette recorder working perfectly well, away from my destructive hands.

"It's a demo reel," Jessica says, slipping the damn thing comfortably into the slot. "The usual sensationalism. You know, effects of NAFTA, globalization, on American jobs, American families. Guess who they targeted? Or rather, which of Clean Earth's factories they decided to investigate?"

There on the screen is Rose, the nurse from yesterday. Seated in a room that—it's almost identical to the room where you did your little performance, Roxanna. And next to Rose on the couch where Jason used to camp out watching TV and do his homework before I dispatched him, there on the couch is a thirteen-year-old kid called Simon. And Rose's brother Eduardo, who lost his job six months ago, along with their mother, Marta, who is not there, they both lost their job when their plant closed. But in the background, grinning at the camera, is Rose's father, Santos Montero, not an ex-marine but a security guard nevertheless, and next to him his best friend José with—what else?—a paralyzed left arm who, of course, lives with them. My family. All so different, all so similar. The models upon which my family was based, Roxanna. The real people somebody studied so you could act out my fantasies. And more than that: because now Rose is protesting what happened to her lover, Johnny, one name that hasn't changed. Nor his fate. "My boyfriend's being held on drug possession," Rose announces plaintively to the camera. "It's a trumped-up charge."

When was that? I want to ask her, that nurse who works in my factory, that nurse who created the role for you, Roxanna. When was your Johnny arrested? Was it before I went to Philadelphia for my therapy? Or did it happen afterward, did it happen to the real Johnny because I had decided to do it first to the actor Johnny, stop him from fucking you, my fictitious Roxanna, in front of my eyes?

I tell the driver to drop me off at Tolgate's.

"Graham!" Jessica shakes her head. "I said you needed help, but I didn't expect you to pop in this morning for a quickie with your shrink. We have to decide what to do about our Philadelphia plant before this segment airs. We've got two weeks. That's all. Once it's out there, we won't be able to sell that derelict operation, not even to Granger. And that woman there, she said they were thinking about a strike. So it's—"

I cut her off as the limo stops in front of the building that houses the Corporate Life Therapy Institute.

"Go ahead to the office," I say to her. "I'll be there in a few minutes. And then we'll fix this mess."

I'm lying.

Where I'm really going is back to Philadelphia.

SIX

"Remember us?"

"Yeah, we're back, Rose. If you
don't mind us calling you that,
Rose, seeing as we're old acquain-
tances."

"Is this about Johnny?"
she says. "I've already told
you people all I know
about—"

"We told you the last time,
Rose, what did we say the last time?
When we came to talk to you about that
friend of yours—Evangelina, right?—about
what seemed to be a suicide?"

"Didn't we say that we're a special unit, that we
don't ask what others like to ask?"

"We hope you don't mind if we film this."

"You can say no, of course, you're within your rights, but
it helps us, you know, like the last time, to have you on tape."

"Go ahead," she says. "But don't expect me to be like last time—I mean, not after what you did to Johnny."

"I hope you're not accusing us of having done anything to Johnny, Rose."

"We'll ignore what you just said. We'll construe it as said in the heat of the moment. You don't want to be on record suggesting we did anything illegal, Rose, I hope that wasn't your intention."

"Johnny was set up," she says. "He's innocent and he was set up. He'd never be involved in anything that could hurt people, drugs or anything like that."

"Well, we're not that interested in Johnny, in fact."

"In fact we'd rather speak about you, Rose."

"And about your father."

"My father?" she says. "What's my father got to—?"

"Drugs, Rose. You're a nurse and you have access to lots of drugs."

"That's ridiculous," she says. "I don't have access to anything of the sort. I deal with my patients by applying balms, brewing them teas, using my fingers to relieve their pain, I—What do you mean, drugs?"

"Well, we'll tell you. It turns out that you've been jumping around jobs for a while now—and all of them could—notice that we're not saying it's so—but it is remarkable how every one of them might have afforded you the chance, you know…"

"The chance to what?" she says.

"You don't mind if we go through some of your employment history, Rose? Just for the record?"

"Let's see, you start when you're not yet sixteen. Summer job. Helped by your father's friend, the one with the lame arm, that old—

"Yeah, that old—what's his name?"

"Who cares? He gets you a job receiving flowers in the old factory from overseas, right? Where you happen to meet your future boyfriend, this Johnny, who's part of the flower delivery business already."

"I hardly noticed him at the time," she says. "We didn't date until much—"

"And you end up being so good at this flower thing that they keep you on during the school year."

"Four hours after school, three times a week, full salary, full benefits. For a girl not yet sixteen. How do you explain that, Rose?"

"It was a perfect fit," she says. "Management understood that the final output, what you extracted from the roses, depended on your willingness to let the flower take its own journey, not accelerate it through synthetic means. They insisted on providers using only natural methods of growth and cultivation. And I had a knack."

"A knack for what?"

"I could tell," she says. "Just by touching the flowers, sniffing them as well, but mostly by touch, measuring with my fingers the weight and consistency of stem and bulb, I was able to tell how good the whole shipment was from a few flowers, that's all I needed to pronounce judgment and figure out which ones we should use immediately and which ones had been kept fresh with spray and chemicals and other ways, so we needed to steam and distill them later and could expect less yield."

"You could just know, just like that? Sounds creepy to me."

"Yeah, it does sound creepy. I'll tell you what, we've got a rose with us. A closed rose. You tell us how good it is, would you do that?"

"On camera, you mean?" she says. "Turn the camera off and I'll do it."

"You don't like being taped? What if a talent scout happened to see you? You could end up on a show or something."

"They already offered me that," she says. "Some time ago. From *The Reality Show*, they said they were. 'Never heard of it,' I said. 'You will, you will,' the man said. 'Are you interested or what?' the lady who was with him said. And I was interested, if I could make some money and—but they never called back. Just a lot of questions, really private, and then a thin thank-you note and a big fat bouquet of flowers, which was sort of cruel, knowing as they did that my mother hates flowers, they sent us some anyway, almost as if they wanted to—I don't know, upset us, me and her."

"Well, we're not from any *Reality Show*, Rose. We'll shut the camera down while you're showing us your thing with the flowers."

"Here it is. Careful, it's…"

"Alright," she says. "This rose, then. It's closed. Tight. How many petals does it have? Because that's what a young rose hides, that's its secret—and the only way for most people to tell is by waiting, watching and waiting and then counting. Or you can use thermometers and machines and chemicals that you drop on the rose in a lab. But none of that really works, because you need to let each rose open gradually, reveal itself at its own pace, take its time, petal by petal, opening to the light that showers onto it, slowly, indolently, *imperceptiblemente*. The way in which the moon rises or changes shape. That's the tempo, that's how long it should take. That's what we should do with a rose, with the food we cook and eat, act toward one another. But of course we don't."

"All this is fascinating, of course, Rose, but maybe you'd—"

"You see," she says. "Just my point. People are impatient, men have learned how to accelerate time, take time and crush it, oil the wheels of time as if it were a machine you could drive faster, make the petals exhibit themselves before they're ready, really ready. This very rose I'm holding in my hand now, you can split and squeeze it into giving up its ghosts, you can stop the flower in midprayer, make it dance for a stranger's eyes, but the flower takes its revenge."

"Its revenge?"

"A rose that's been exposed artificially to prying eyes," she says, "won't give the oil or the fragrance it might have, its color won't soothe the eyes as it should. A rose that's been pushed and cajoled, its legs and arms opened wide, crucified for anybody to see, made vulnerable, that rose will mask its deepest secret, even if it fools you into thinking it has submitted to you. This rose, for instance—it has only eight petals. Not more."

"Only eight?"

"That's not very much. Not taking into account what we paid for this rose."

"Well, you were tricked," she says. "Leave it in water, go on, count the petals as they appear and in a week's time you'll see if I'm right."

"Well, we don't have the luxury of waiting that long, Rose, so I'm going to assume you're right."

"Yeah, we're going to give you the benefit of the doubt."

"Assuming you have this *knack*, as you call it, well, then, how do you do it?"

"I'm not sure myself," she says. "I think it was my mother who taught me back when she didn't hate flowers, I think that when I touched each flower here in the States, I was also contacting the fingers that had said good-bye to the flowers back there, not only in Colombia but anywhere that the flowers had been planted and nursed and packaged, the fingers of women and girls like me and my mother back in the country where I had been born, it's as if they'd left their fingerprints, their finger-whisperings on the stalk and outer leaves."

"Finger-whisperings? You're a poet, you know that, Rose? You're a real poet."

"But I still don't understand how you do it."

"People forget," she says, "that the smell from a flower, a rose, for instance, it's what we value most but for the rose it's garbage, it's a way of getting rid of what it doesn't need, it's how the rose grows, like we do, you know, by ridding ouselves of what we don't need. Sweat, saliva, other things. Dreams during the night. If you don't love people's garbage, you'll never understand them, it's a way of knowing what they've got inside, what they're harboring, through the waste they throw out of their houses or their bodies or their minds, you have to really know the plants, know them *desde adentro*, as if from inside. And that's what I knew, that first summer before I was sixteen, before I had ever fallen in love, I knew when a flower wasn't ready because its readiness was imposed upon it by some unfamiliar and unloving hand. I knew when to send it on its way so its floral essence could cure and calm, not only people but dogs, horses, everything that breathes. That's when I was happiest in the world."

"So why did you stop?"

"Hold it, hold it. Are we done with the demonstration? Because if we're done, I'd like to start the cameras again, that's if our Rose here doesn't mind. Good. So now, why didn't you stay in that job forever if it made you so happy?"

"Because of my mother," she says. "I asked to be transferred to Herbs and Herbal Teas, to make her feel good, my mother. I thought, well, I could still work with flowers in a way, jasmine and chamomile and hibiscus, even if they were all cut up and dried and steamed out by the time they got to me, they could no longer really be considered live flowers speaking to my fingers, but even that wasn't enough, that I'd left those carnations and roses and chrysanthemums that made my mother so nervous, even that didn't make her happy. I spent, all told, eight years in the milling room—that's where we blend and test and adjust and then we sift—you know deep-six the tough stalks or the fiber—to make sure all the teas have the same pure consistency, the same flavor. But even that wasn't enough."

"She hated flowers?"

"My mother," she says, "believes that flowers are a curse on the family. She thinks flowers have plagued us like insects or like a pesticide. *Pesticida*, she says, hissing every syllable at my father. *Una maldición*. And my own daughter! And then in Spanish, with contempt, *la niña de las flores. Mi propia hija*. The Flower Girl! And afterward she turns her head away from me, looks in the mirror, and I know she's seeing the woman she might have been, the Marta that might have been, if not for the flowers, she says."

"Why's that, Rose? Was she—well, born that way? You know, some people, my grandmother for instance, she had hay-fever, she would... Is that what—?"

"My mother wasn't always like that," she says. "When we moved from Catalina—"

"How old were you then?"

"Eight," she says. "We moved because my mamá had heard they were cultivating carnations for export in the Sabana de Bogotá and were looking for strong young women to work in the greenhouses—and that's what she did. Damn flowers got me into this mess, she would say, flowers and poetry on your father's sweet lips—and flowers will get us out, we'll follow the trail of those *claveles* and *margaritas* and *crisante-mos* all the way north. So you can see that she bore the flowers a grudge, but didn't really hate them, at that point imagined she could get the better of them, outwit *las flores malditas.*"

"But it didn't work out that way?"

"Are you sure you're interested in—?" she says. "Look, she did just about every job there was to do in the *floricultura* industry there in Fanza on the Sabana de Bogotá—she bored holes in the soil, she plant-ed bulb by bulb, she made sure the stalks were straight by building lat-tices of string, she shed the shunted dry buds one by one, she even worked in the refrigeration chambers at the very end and was so weak that she got pneumonia. They sent her there because of the dizziness and—are you sure you—?"

"We'll tell you when we want you to stop talking, Rose."

"Let us decide what we want to hear. You just tell us about your mother. When she started to feel dizzy."

"First it was the headaches," she says, "like her head was being cracked open with a rat crawling up her spine into her head, creeping up and up, *el dolor me muerde, me muerde,* she'd say, which means the pain was eating her, biting her, and my hands would try and help her, I would massage her head in the evenings and she would fall asleep, her head in my hands like a baby being rocked, but I couldn't do any-thing against the fainting spells that came next. And the flower-com-pany doctor—he said it was laziness, that she should go back to work. Until finally the women all complained, she and the other women had discovered that it was the chemicals used in the fumigation, most of the workers were sick by then, because the chemicals are always there, in the land first to make it clean of infestations and then dur-ing the irrigation and then when you're picking the carnations and later especially the chemicals stick to you, to your hair, to your breasts and get through the *tejido* of your clothes and into your shoes and even past your mask, which is supposed to protect you, that was the worst moment, according to mamá, when she was lifting the flowers up to make bunches and tie them together with rubber bands and grade them, she would end up drenched."

"We get the idea."

"Well, you wanted to know," she says. "She'd come home and try to rub the taste from her skin, she—'Soft petals for poets and weddings,' she'd say, scrubbing over and over again, making me pour water and then go and get some more from the well, 'Sickness for me and the others. All the color's in the flowers,' she'd say, 'while us—look at me, pale, pale, pale. *Pálidas.* I could die for all the *crisantemos* cared.' And she probably would have died if papá had not right then—it was a miracle, God must have taken pity on us, pity on Eduardo, he was thirteen years old at that time and had left school and started to work with his quick little hands in the flower fields, and I was only ten, but maybe they would have accepted me as well, if just then papá hadn't made the final payment on our tickets and the visa came through as if Somebody were smiling on us from heaven."

"You pray a lot to God, Rose?"

"Yes," she says.

"And does it work?"

"You don't pray for things to work," she says. "But I don't think this is any of your business, to tell you the truth."

"Well, you've convinced us, Rose."

"About your mother. We understand why she wasn't enthusiastic about you working with flowers, why you felt you had to change jobs. But there's one thing we don't understand. About the packages."

"Yes, Rose, those packages you get from Colombia. We've heard you use whatever's in them for your ointments, your own brews. How come your mother doesn't object to that?"

"Yes, Rose, why doesn't she object to your getting packages from Colombia?"

"Lots of people get packages from Colombia," she says.

"Not every person who gets a package has a boyfriend who delivers flowers packed with drugs inside. Not every person who gets a package worked in a lab like you did."

"I only worked there one year," she says.

"Not enough drugs there, Rose? Is that why you quit?"

"I'm getting tired of this," she says. "If this goes on, I'm not talking anymore, not unless a lawyer is present."

"Now that would really look suspicious, Rose."

"Yeah, we thought you didn't have anything to hide. And now you threaten us with lawyers and things like that when we're having a friendly conversation, just the three of us here."

"After all, you did go work in a lab, Rose. Why did you do that?"

"Is this the last question?" she says.

"Almost."

"I wanted to change jobs," she says. "People around me are like gardens, after all. You tend to their body like you water a plant, you trim it, you make sure it gets lots of sun, you pray for it. If I couldn't care for the flowers, I'd be a nurse."

"Strange way to do it, going to a lab first."

"Paul St. Martin, the manager of our factory, suggested it," she says, "when I told him my plans. He was—well, pleased with me, with my work, and thought I could do better for myself in the lab. 'Tell you what,' Mr. St. Martin said. 'Try the lab for a year and if you don't like it, the company will train you as a nurse.' And I—the truth is I was curious. Because of blue."

"Your favorite color."

"Yes," she says, "I'd heard they were producing—I don't know if that's the word, creating maybe—creating, producing, they were making roses blue. I wanted to see how they did it, even if I was dead against blue roses. I still am. If God would have wanted roses to be blue, He'd have made them blue, right? So I assisted them with that. And with other stuff, experiments. They showed me how they isolate the gene, splice and manipulate the gene that determines why something, anything is blue, and then they find ways of going back and putting it into the rose seed, the plasma. The seeds came from Colombia and arrived in refrigerated boxes and I took them out and I spoke to them, greeted them when they came out, and they were glad to see me, but I wasn't happy to see them. I knew that when they returned to their country, they'd have been altered, would grow blue back there."

"So what's the gimmick, Rose?"

"Yeah, Rose, what's in it for the Company?"

"They get a fee for each blue flower grown and exported all over the world," she says.

"Smart."

"You should've stayed there, Rose. You'd be rich now. Swimming in it. Maybe you could have kept your boyfriend and your father out of trouble."

"My father?" she says.

"Yeah, your father."

"What about him?" she says.

"Don't get all defensive. We're just doing our job."

"He's a good man," she says.

"Then it won't be hard to clear up any doubts we have about him, right? One or two little points here and there?"

"Like…?" she says.

"Like why he left his country the night you were born, I think you said last time if I'm not mistaken? That somebody wanted to kill him."

"Yes, Rose, what was your father so scared of?"

"I don't know," she says. "Why don't you ask him?"

"We have, Rose, we have. And now we're asking you."

"What did he answer?" she says.

"He said he had problems with his in-laws, with the people in that town—Catalina? Had to leave in a hurry. Seems they didn't like him because he'd fallen in love with your mother, a local girl, seems she had been really young when he… you know."

"That's as much as we've been able to get out of him."

"We thought you might know something else, Rose."

"I don't," she says.

"You mean you've never asked him why he wasn't there for your birth, your own father?"

"No," Rose says. "Never."

THIRD PART

For I have seen a briar through winter's snows
rattle its tough and menacing bare stems,
and then, in season, open its pale rose;

—DANTE, PARADISO, CANTO XIII, 133–135

SEVEN

Take notes, miss.
Patient: Graham Blake.
Said patient, still under treatment, burst into my office when
I was in the middle of an evaluation session with —just
put X. Fortunately X was
not somebody Graham Blake
knew, so confidentiality has been
maintained in this matter, but we
underestimated the degree of rage that
said patient Graham Blake would develop
in this stage of his therapy. I continue to con-
sider him fundamentally nonviolent, but it
remains to be seen where his agitation may lead him.

I hustled X out of the room, gave him assurances
that our session would resume in fifteen minutes, turned
to Graham Blake, who could barely contain himself. As soon
as the door shut and we were alone, said patient began to rant.

I wish I had been foresightful enough to have pressed the Record button when he walked in, but now he was looking straight at me, staring at my finger, daring me to proceed, daring me to make a move, and I felt a slight tremor of fear. No. Correction. Cross out fear. Apprehension is a better word. Looks better if these notes are ever published in my book on the Tolgate syndrome. In fact, miss, don't transcribe that last phrase about a tremor. Makes me look like… Just note my interchange with said patient.

His tirade consisted of a series of comments and questions and insults, one after the other. I can't recall them all, but here goes a good approximation. "Why didn't you tell me my family was alive? My family, the real one, the one you modeled the fake one on, don't tell me you didn't, you bastard. In Philadelphia. Rose Montero. And her brother just like Jason. And her father just like Bud. You want more? You want more? What sort of mindgame are you playing, Tolgate?"

I was about to open my mouth to inform him that this was not a game and that neither he nor I were playing, but he grabbed me by the collar and sat me down forcibly.

"I want clear answers and I want them now. First question: Are all therapy sessions with actors? Or are there also sessions with real people?"

I followed the advice of our manual: Be logical and, above all, never forget you are dealing with businessmen.

"You think I would go to the trouble of doing this with real people when I can get actors? Which do you think is less risky, less expensive? Which of the two groups do you think I can keep under tighter control? Which of the two options creates more employment and fewer lawsuits, is more responsive to the whims of clients?"

"So nobody ever had a session with my original family, the real one? Nobody ever manipulated them from across a glass mirror, through a camera, nobody ever did anything irreparable to them?"

"People have done plenty of irreparable things to them, to the Montero family. More powerful people are always doing things to those with less power, Mr. Blake, but the way you mean it, directly, spying on them, hounding them, playing God—no, that's never happened to the Monteros, never the way it happened, we made you believe it was happening, to Roxanna's folks."

"When did Johnny—the real one—get framed for using drugs?"

"Who says he was framed?"

"Rose, his girlfriend. In Philly. Don't play mind-fucking games with me, Tolgate. You admit that you used that family as a model, you admit that, don't you?"

"Of course I do. Not only them. The Monteros served merely as a preliminary basis for the script we were working on, what we call the central core. From that we improvise, change the country of origin, create composites, let the actors and actresses find the right tone. Depending, of course, on who the patient is, what he or she needs."

"Women are patients as well?"

Blake was beginning to calm down, miss. He was asking a question that was not relevant to his dilemma. He was beginning to be intellectually curious. A good sign. I indicated a chair. He sat down. It was the armchair he always used when he showed up for evaluation sessions, the one he had chosen to sit in the first time Sam Halneck sent him to the Institute.

"No women so far," I answered. "I say he or she out of deference to contemporary sensitivity."

"Why no women patients, then?"

"Maybe because there are so few female executives. Maybe because they're harder to fool. I don't think our Sonia could handle somebody like, say, your wife. Your former wife. Like Sonia handled you, I mean."

Perhaps not a smart comment, miss. To call attention to the fact that he had been fooled. But said patient has a rather high concept of himself and I wished to remind him that he may not be as smart and clever as he seems to think.

"So why that particular family for me?" he asked. "Why the Monteros in Philadephia?"

I cleared my throat, gave myself time. "I'm really not at liberty to discuss why I chose them. It would disclose the way in which we planned for you, and that would have a negative impact on your therapy."

"You said I was cured. So you can tell me."

"You don't seem cured right now. You seem rather agitated."

"Agitated? I should be throwing the motherfucking desk out that window and throw you out along with it. I should be reporting you to the police."

"First time that I heard it's illegal to present a month-long play for the enjoyment of a rich patron. We knew we weren't doing anything wrong. Can you say the same thing about yourself, Mr. Blake? By all means, call the police."

"How about the fact that you spied on a real family. That's invasion of privacy."

"You'd have a hard time proving that, I think. Really, Mr. Blake, what's wrong with our having based your fictitious family on a real living contemporary one? Didn't it enhance the reality for you? Didn't it work? And who was hurt?"

"You can't just spy on people like that, take their lives and turn them into the core, as you say, of someone else's drama. Their lives— damn it, those lives belong to them."

I was ready for that objection. You've heard it, miss, I've heard it so many times that I'm beginning to tire of it.

"Artists do it all the time," I replied. "We're therapy artists. We take reality, we exaggerate it a bit, we cast the parts, we organize a perfect spectacle with one member in the audience: participatory theater at three million dollars the ticket and an extremely comfortable seat. A perfect and unrepeatable work of art, high-class interactive soap opera, all the more unique because it never goes beyond that one individual. One product, one consumer, one customer, one treatment. No bastardized, common denominator, mass culture here. And nobody is harmed."

"You keep saying that. You keep saying it. But there's somebody who is hurt: Johnny. Maybe you had him framed before I ever came on the scene, you had that guy busted on false drug charges to see how the family would react, to measure how they'd take it, how that Rose woman would take it. And then Sonia convinced me to do the same thing. That's one possibility."

"Your imagination has not diminished one little bit, Mr. Blake, since I had the pleasure to watch you consummate your wishes. Your wishes, not ours."

But he wasn't listening at this point, miss, to any of my attempts to placate him.

"The other possibility," our patient Graham Blake went on monomaniacally, "is that the real Johnny was busted after I ordered the actor, the fake one, arrested. In that case, I'm really responsible, I mean directly responsible: it was my idea you decided to put into action for some perverse reason that I—why did you do it? Why did you frame him?"

"All patients swear by the infallibility of their shrinks. But we are less superhuman than you presume. If I had that sort of power... And you still haven't proven that this Johnny was framed. Who's to say he isn't guilty? And why should you care? You don't even know him."

"You're not answering my questons. Was my family only used for me? Or have other corporate patients played with them as well?"

"Surely you're not jealous of the parallel dramas we arrange for other patients. What we do for them, with them, what models we handle, is entirely our business and entirely dependent on the sort of problems and dilemmas they bring to the sessions. For that sort of revenue, we tailor our stories, our cast. Of course, we prefer to offer exclusivity, but if we find that a character employed in one situation is exactly the one we need for another situation, for another client, we would quite naturally never hesitate to resort to that source of inspiration. When you've found a winning formula... Is it any different in your line of business? But again, Mr. Blake, I ask you: Why do you care? Aren't you cured?"

And then said patient finally announced what I had been hoping he would announce when he burst in, evidence that he was well on his way to the next stage in his therapy. Proof that it was all working the way it should. He said, "It's different if my family is real. If their pain is real. If their hope is real."

And I responded as I must at this time, I responded what I always do to anyone who comes this far: "It doesn't matter," I said, "if they're real or not. What's real is the moral choice. You made the right one back there when you defied all the rules, demeaned yourself, endangered your status and maybe even your safety, to save Roxanna. Without knowing she was an actress. For you she was real. She was in trouble and you broke down all the barriers—with a little help from us of course—to rescue her."

"And now she's in trouble again. Not her. Rose. The first one. The real one. She's in trouble. The factory's in danger. Her father is still a man who could do anything to her. And her lover is in jail. They're all in trouble."

He had been building up to that revelation and I had been waiting for him to reach it, miss. He needed me to say what I then said, he needed in some subconscious way, my authorization.

I gave it to him.

"Go to Philadelphia, then, if they're in such danger. Save them all over again. But if I were you, I wouldn't. There are millions of families as screwed up as that one, most of them even more screwed up, all over the world. Graham. You can't save them all."

He stood up.

"I don't need to save them all, Dr. Tolgate," he said. "One family," he said. "That's all I need to do: save that one family."

And he was gone.

One final observation, miss. Please ask technical services if there is some way, were this situation ever to repeat itself, for a recording device to automatically kick in. It's very inconvenient not to be able to examine the patient's face at my leisure, extrapolate from his voice and expression what his next steps might conceivably be.

Would you be so good as to have these notes typed and on my desk by this afternoon, miss?

Thank you.

That will be all.

EIGHT

You would be proud of me, Roxanna.
I followed in your footsteps.
You must have watched her for
many days, picked up some of her
gestures, studied the way she
walked and prayed and smiled
—how on earth did you manage
to imitate Rose's smile so perfectly?
You couldn't have managed, I'm sure, if
you hadn't done it yourself, personally, I
mean, it couldn't have been enough to study
videos that so-called Ivan or some other muscle
boy for Tolgate amassed for your benefit. I am sure
you did this up close, nearby, spent hours tailing her,
maybe even got to know her at The Sad Dogs, that Irish bar
she spends so much time at, maybe even had a drink together
like I did, and more than one.

Did you rent a car at the airport and drive to the Clean Earth factory and wait for her to emerge? Maybe you didn't need to, maybe you live in this city—local talent, right?—maybe Tolgate got you a job inside the plant to be able to stalk her, cozy up. I can't do that: The managers have met me—I can take my phobia against public appearances just so far, after all— so I couldn't call Paul St. Martin up, demand that he give a certain Gus Henderson a position in the cafeteria. That's the name I registered under at an amiable bed and breakfast in the old Chestnut Hill neighborhood where I was born, brought up: Gus Henderson, traveling salesman dealing with surveillance technology, providing homes and offices with bugging devices, hidden microphones, tiny cameras, uplinks to satellites and internet spy-browsers. That's what I told Mrs. O'Leary at the reception desk: so she wouldn't question all the equipment that would be carried up to my room, installed there. Everything paid in cash. No tracking me down, Jessica, Tolgate, Sam. Not till I'm good and ready, Granger, you son of a bitch.

She rides a bike, Roxanna. Rose does. You didn't incorporate that detail into your performance, didn't even mention it once. You made yourself out to be a walking freak, somebody who covers miles and miles on foot, does not take the bus or the metro unless it is absolutely imperative, would never buy a car even if she could afford it. I should have had my doubts: How did you make it back home so fresh if you'd been hitting the sidewalks that much? I didn't think of those details— or I may have simply presumed our side-to-side apartments were around the corner from the factory. I was too absorbed in what you choreographed for me, what Tolgate made you dance, to go into the nitty-gritty. Whereas with Rose—it's all nitty-gritty, all minutiae. I've been extra careful, observant, had to. I'm on my own. One mistake and I could have blown it.

Not one mistake.

I took my time, just as you would have recommended, as your character based on Rose would have insisted. The reward will come, you said to your Johnny with your eyes, as you kept on putting off the act of love, forced him to enjoy the everlasting foreplay. My own reward came after several hours in that rented car listening to Bruce Springsteen go on and on about "Born in the USA": There she was, biking out of the factory, the wind flapping at that dress. The same dress you had worn, Roxanna, when I first saw you, so similar to the blue dress I plundered from Natasha's body while the hidden cameras rolled.

I've become suspicious, Roxanna: You taught me that too. And I wondered at that being the very dress. That special blue. It meant, of course, that the costume designer of the show you and Tolgate and the rest put on for me had been inspired by the real-life Rose, that designer had copied her clothing like you copied her life, the tide of her life. But it could mean something else: It could mean that Rose was in Tolgate's pay, that he had warned her ahead of time to wear precisely that dress to complete the circle of my seduction. Too much of a coincidence, I thought to myself, under the thrill of watching those legs of Rose's, which were so distinct from your legs and yet pumping at the bike with such casual abandon, reminding me of the common bonds, the common core that joins you both in spite of the difference. Too much of a coincidence: alarm bells. What if Rose had been part of this conspiracy from the start? Not spied upon but informer. Not watched in secret but debriefed daily, a consultant on the project, critiquing the way you sigh, Roxanna, when you make love. "That's not how I'd do it; listen to me, imitate me, try to be me when you make love." I can hear Rose's voice offering advice. Advice she never gave. She is the real thing, Roxanna, definitely did not participate in your sham, does not know that you took over her existence to cure the owner of her factory.

But at that point I couldn't be sure, so I mused upon this possibility as I followed her down the slow streets of Philadelphia to a building that reminded me of the one I entered to save you that day you supposedly were committing suicide: similar, but not identical. Like everything else. Rose's home. Not on the eighth floor, but four stories up. I should know: I've been up those stairs so many times. I've been to dinner, even to Sunday breakfast/brunch just yesterday. The Monteros showered me with the hospitality that you never offered this guest, Roxanna. But then, on the other hand, this guest never gave you anything in return either, did I? Except trouble.

I made amends for that, made sure the very same evening that I would be a benefactor and not a destroyer. I sent up a bottle of whiskey and a cheesecake and added a basket of gourmet food. Signed the card: *An admirer from near and far.* Thought that was rather smart of me. Smarter still: The goodies were all things the Monteros cherished. You and your false family, Roxanna, giving me the right information about the true likes, dislikes, of the people you were modeled on. A seduction is always easier when you know everything ahead of time—even if Tolgate prissily disagrees with the word *everything*—about the object of your affections. I had been, for instance, about to purchase fifty roses and then remembered something in the dossier Sonia retrieved on the screen, something about how Rose's mother hated flowers—so I didn't make that mistake. And no caviar. You all hate caviar. I had to suppose that Tolgate had pillaged that fact from the real-life Monteros—and confirmed later, when I was invited to dinner, that they do detest caviar. I brought up the subject. Too pretentious, Marta complained. Too bourgeois, said Eduardo. Too much cholesterol, Rose said.

Though before I sat down to Marta's home cooking, I had already verified that both families had the same tastes, knew that Rose and her family had been delighted with my present. And intrigued. Because I had waited on the landing outside the fourth-floor corridor, had bribed the delivery boy to give me feedback. A tip larger than a week's salary and he was in my hands. He came down the stairs with me and passed on every detail. I watched them through his eyes that tarried and lingered and lapped up the puzzled and joyful reactions to my gift.

Not the last gift. Next morning, early, before Roxanna and her father left for work, I sent them a mammoth television set. What they couldn't know was that I had ordered a surveillance shop to equip the set with a tiny video camera and transmitter so that as soon as they plugged it in, I was able to survey their living room. Not as downbeat and grimy as the apartment your Dr. Tolgate had established for my viewing enjoyment, cleaner, more dignified, but the same air about it. Again, the set designer of your fake apartment, Roxanna, must have canvassed Rose's residence, assessed it, repeated most of the features, for instance that couch where Jason once slept, where Simon now stretches out his sleeping bag when you banish him from the room you share.

Simon was the most enthusiastic of all with the new television set. You were worried. I watched you through the monitor from my bed-and-breakfast colonial bedroom and saw the furrows on your forehead. You didn't like this, these presents from that faraway and nearby admir-er, you inferred who would have to pay with her body for those atten-tions. You. I said you. I mean her. I mean Rose. She was worried.

Her mother, Marta, was just as anxious. "We should return it," she said. "When you're poor and a gift comes, especially if it's flowers, it's always a woman who ends up taking care of the debt." Marta, by the way, does not have a Puerto Rican food stand or anything of the sort. In fact they're from Colombia and the food street thing was an invention of Tolgate's or maybe the actress performing the mother's role came up with that or perhaps they decided on that idea because it was an easy way to get me to intervene against her, make Silvia an appetizing tar-get. Marta can't be hurt like that because she still hasn't found a job: too old, too unqualified, too grumpy. Rose's brother Eduardo, however, was a gambler just like Ned had been, and he, of course, was on Simon's side, only they couldn't agree on what they should see that evening. Eduardo wanted to watch the races on a giant screen, the kid wanted to tune in to the NCAA tournament. But Rose's father—his name is Santos—thought that it would be better to sell the damn thing. The family needed the money more than it needed another TV set. There was an ensuing confrontation—something about how Santos wanted the money for drink and Marta was not going to let him have it and they were at each other's throats, just like old times. Playing their aggression out again, again for my pleasure, except that now nobody had written their lines beforehand, now they were playing their real lives, she complaining about some poems he had written her, he reciting one of the poems back at her in Spanish, telling her to lighten up. While Rose breathed deeply and tried to make believe she was somewhere else.

They ended up selling the damn thing. That very evening. So I had only that day to take advantage of it. Not really. There was nobody there. When I was watching your apartment, Roxanna, the production team was always heedful to have somebody around, to entertain me, I guess, in order to drop hints about their behavior, what they wanted, what they feared, always keep the action going. Now I spent ten hours gazing at an empty room, without even one of the Monteros coming home, not because they forgot something, wanted to cook lunch, play a game of cards, bogus pretexts they used to make up to fill my days while I waited for you to float through the door. My TV screen now blank of people. That's what happens in real life, when nobody is preselecting the juiciest scenes, when there's not a Dr. Tolgate who wants to make sure his patient is hooked and anxious to get involved. Even the dialogue that morning at breakfast while they discussed the television set's destiny was chaotic and meandering, full of references to people I didn't know and incomprehensible inside jokes in dire need of major editing. And impenetrable words in Spanish that only Cervantes himself could have deciphered. Get to the point, I kept on muttering to the screen—until finally they did. Santos banged his hand on the table and said *Basta, carajo!* Enough of this. I celebrated the finality of the gesture only to be disappointed by what he immediately decreed: the set would be sold that very day. They needed the dough. And no more arguing about this, *entendieron?*

I did take advantage of the bare and vacant day to figure out how to proceed, again I needed to come up with a game plan. I thought of you, Roxanna, and your patience, the rhythm that you had learned perhaps from Rose or perhaps was part of your own outlook, the patience I needed if I was to succeed. Wasn't the family's absence a chance to wire the apartment? I went to the surveillance company's office and convinced the manager that I was the owner of the apartment. All it took was doubling the fee and we had a deal, they broke in the next day and installed hidden cameras in each room. And by the next night, I was in business, could watch every movement of the family.

I had already made some progress on other fronts. I was, of course, waiting for Rose outside her workplace. This time she didn't go straight home, but biked to the Sad Dogs for a drink. You didn't drink alcohol, Roxanna—probably in order to purify your image, make you more saintly, more of a challenge to corrupt. Rose, on the other hand, likes her liquor, likes it strong. She doesn't smoke, at least that's something. And she does pray on and off, though less New Age stuff than straight Catholic pleas to God. That evening, listening to her speak to a couple of bar buddies, I heard her explain how her prayers really had an effect—if she prayed for someone, that person did measurably better than if she didn't. Her friends were skeptical: Get Johnny out of the can, then, Flower Girl, save the factory, wave your magic wand, Bippi-ty-Boppity-Boo—but she stuck to her guns. Stuck to her guns and ordered another Jack Daniel's.

I stayed as far from her as I could, merely passing as closely as I could from time to time when her back was turned and she was engrossed in conversation. I listened to her with my own back turned in the noisy bar, thought to myself how easy this was going to be, almost too easy.

What could be simpler than to follow her later to the city jail where Johnny is detained? She came out after an hour, looking distraught, dejected. But just like you, Roxanna, she's a winner. Or so I said to myself: Rose is not going to let herself be beaten. She'll always bounce back.

With a little help from this friend. That night I made a mental note: explore the Johnny question, secure a lawyer for him, win his case. That's right, Roxanna. Even if Johnny's arrest turned out not to be my responsibility, I was going to intervene on his behalf anyway. Undo what

I had done or what Tolgate had done or destiny, who cared who had screwed Johnny over—I would fix it once and for all.

The next evening I made my move on Rose. Gratifying as it was to have that view from my bed and breakfast of the comings and goings of the family, that pleasure could be enormously heightened by transforming myself into an active member of the family, go beyond being a mere spectator. What d'you think of that, huh, Tolgate? Is that normally what someone with your famous Syndrome would do? Look at me, infiltrating the Monteros, dropping behind Rose's line of defense. All without your indulgence, Doctor Tolgate, or tight-assed Sonia's consent, for that matter. All a man needs is imagination, imagination and a good stash of dollar bills.

I paid off a kid to steal Rose's bike. Yes, Roxanna, scheming as usual, turning this into a movie, I know, but that's what I'm good at, even that bastard Hank Granger would have felt a tinge of admiration at my ingenuity. I told the kid just when he had to do it: As she unchained the bike, as she began to tinker with the lock—that's when. He grabbed it in a dash and then, as agreed, slowed down just enough so I could catch him, drag him back screaming insults, the kid really overdid it, but Rose didn't seem to notice his ham acting. She was looking at me with gratitude and it turned to something deeper, more compelling, it turned into respect, when I obeyed her entreaties and let the kid go, didn't take him to the police.

"I don't believe," I said to Rose, "in punishment as a way of dealing with people who make mistakes, especially if they're young."

"Well, I don't either. Compassion goes farther."

"So what do we do with this kid? Maybe he could work in your garden, pay it off that way."

"I don't have a garden," Rose answered with a smile. A sorrowful one. Maybe she wants, just like you did, to go back to her country. Maybe that was her dream, I thought: to spend her life cultivating herbs, sending them out with her prayers. And all she needs is a bit of capital, a helping hand.

"Well, we won't press charges this time," I said. "We've all done something wrong when we were his age. Didn't you?"

She looked at me as if I could read her mind, her past.

"Nobody's perfect," she said, and smiled at me again, but the sorrow had evaporated.

"Some people are close to perfect," I answered. And meant it. And... I wasn't acting, Roxanna. Maybe that's why it all came out so naturally: Because this is me, this is Graham Blake, the real one, the one you'd be proud of. Who believes that we should be spending all that money on schools, instead of prisons. I said so to her and she nodded and I suggested a drink if she had time and she said yes. There's always time, she said. We run out of time, but time doesn't run out on us, not if we treat it with respect.

She liked me. You never gave me a chance, Sonia never gave us a chance, Tolgate erected all those barriers. But Rose cut through every wall as if it were transparent: She has a directness, a... what can I call it? A weight, I guess, that you never had, that maybe you have in your everyday life when you strip yourself of the role you're performing. By weight I mean something you can touch, that has gravitational force. She's—real. I didn't have the impression, not for a moment, that she was a film star. Even though something warned me in my mind, that her straightforward, factual reality would be irresistible and tantalizing for someone like me at this precise moment of what Tolgate kept on calling my ongoing therapy. If she were being paid, I mean. If she were also part of this game Tolgate's got going, that's how he'd have programmed her: as irrestibly real. Though she'd have to be a really top-notch performer, better than you were, and you were the best, Roxanna.

Over some whiskey I let her inform me about Johnny. How he'd been framed, they'd hidden a drug shipment in the flowers from Mexico that he delivers. Though she hadn't witnessed his arrest by the pigs, she said.

"When was that?" I asked, hoping the answer would absolve me. It did.

"Four months ago," she said.

One month before I had appeared on the scene! So I wasn't the one who had done it to him, though his ordeal could still have been commandeered by Tolgate experimenting with the family he would model my therapy on. How long had Tolgate known that I would be his patient? How long had he been spying on me, gathering information on Rose and her buoyant optimism, waiting for me to fall into his clutches?

I sprinkled some real hope into her mix of optimism that evening in the bar. I was well connected, I said, implied that I was a journalist, mentioned a couple of names—all people that Rose would be unable to contact, would never be able to track down to check whether I was lying. I added that this Johnny affair sounded like a major scandal and that it should be investigated. I was willing to help out. At first she was subdued, didn't react as I'd expected. She'd already tried to call attention, she said, to all of this: she'd been filmed by a TV program, four hours of taping. She'd seen the final tape, and all that they'd left were a few snippets here and there, and she'd been so hopeful and now thought it wouldn't make any difference, even if somebody saw the damn program, it would be forgotten tomorrow, it would be swallowed up by indifference, it—

I interrupted her, told her that I would personally speak to these friends of mine in the media, she had to believe me that I could help.

And then, yes, a light flared up in her eyes, a sparkle that reminded me of what I had seen in yours, Roxanna, when I rescued you from death—fake death in that case, maybe fake admiration. Hers, in any case, Rose's I mean, was spontaneous: Nobody had coached her, she hadn't been asked to cry in front of a casting director, try out lines while Tolgate took notes, made comments to Sonia, perhaps comments to somebody else more powerful, that shadow man interested in weakening my sanity, Granger may have looked at you while you worked on looking me deep in the eyes proclaiming my altruism and grace, Tolgate measured your breasts for sure, your ass, wondered how soon he could get his hands on them, pitied me, that fool Graham Blake who would desire it all from behind his glass partition, the way in which the audience looks up at the blank enormous eye of the screen that fills with women we can only touch in our minds, make love to in our imagination.

But you would be wrong, Roxanna, if you deduced from what I'm telling you that I wanted to fuck Rose. Not at all. I may be fascinated with her, but it is a curiously sexless affair, like discovering a long-lost sister, as if she were some sort of daughter. And the woman's a bit on the vulgar side, if you know what I mean. Ingested too much garlic in her life. No. It's you I'd like to ball. Or my Natasha while your image flickers endlessly on a colossal screen above my bed. Rose? I want to save her. And I'm going to save her. When the time is ripe.

We warmed to each other, at any rate, at the Sad Dogs. She downed a bit more than she should have, was leaning against me as I steered her home, pretending that I had no idea where she lived. I steered her, and her bike I steered, trundling down the Philadelphia streets, Gus and Rose and the bike, almost hand in hand.

I helped her up to the apartment, fourth floor, no elevator, introduced myself to the family. They're nicer than your family, the sham members of your sham family, I mean, Roxanna. Spend more time having fun. They pulled up a chaotic chair, sat me down, shared their dinner with me. With me and two other friends who dropped by, just like that, without asking. Where seven can eat, eight can eat, Santos said. And where eight can eat... Nine, said Simon. And where nine can eat... Ten, they all chirped up, as if in a chorus. That's another difference, Roxanna: Their bad luck, the fact that Eduardo's gambled away a major sum of money, the fact that only two of them are working at the moment, the fact that the mortgage is due and they'll have to refinance and no bank will give them a loan for that—none of it seems to dampen their spirit. If anybody tends to be on the manic depressive side, it's Rose; she's the one who feels their pain too deeply. The others... And there are tons of others, by the way. Friends, neighbors, bastketball pals, the cop from his beat, a nosy postman, the union leaders who are organizing a strike soon, bowling partners, yes, all we menfolk went bowling and boozing one night. I do understand why Tolgate decided not to surround your family with all those extras. It would have been distracting. And expensive. He served me up a rather intimate film about a dysfunctional family—based paradoxically on a family that functions quite well and that is not at all intimate. On the contrary. They're extroverts, the lot of them, more typically Latin American than your family was, Roxanna, though I can only recognize the difference now that I've had the chance to visit the real thing, now that I'm free to do whatever I really want with them, the power to make their lives better or worse.

Better, of course, is my plan. But not right away. I don't want them liking me because I overwhelm them with gifts or because their good luck happens to coincide with the moment when I trickled into their lives. I want them to like me because of me. Santos already does. And I must tell you, Roxanna, that I resent how Sonia and Tolgate invented a child-abusing father out to rape his daughter, all that nonsense, to get me riled up, make me jealous. Santos hasn't touched that girl. As you can tell, I'm fond of him. Even if I realize that he's welcomed me because he senses—with the instinct of any immigrant who has crossed a whole continent on foot and survived, who had to run for his life from the town where he married Rose's mother, but I'm getting away from the main point I was trying to make and that is that Santos is aware that I'm his ticket out of here, that my obvious infatuation with his daughter will end up providing some sort of dividends for the family. But even if it didn't, I think he'd like me.

Precisely why I'm not about to provide anything too soon, as I said. It's no sweat to rack up a couple of jobs for Eduardo and Marta, for instance, but that would disturb the delicate equilibrium that now reigns in the household. I prefer Rose to be as vulnerable and needy as when I found her, neither more, nor less.

There are some things, of course, I have already done for her. I called up a prominent lawyer on a pay phone, disguised my voice, suggested a hefty retainer if he represented our Johnny, I needed that young man free within a week or so. He asked me to send him a check and he would look into the matter. An hour later five thousand dollars, in cash, was sitting on his desk, sent by courier. One hour after that I gave him another call. He had agreed, of course, to take the case. "Your friend Johnny," the lawyer drawled, "is guilty as hell. Like most of the other poor bastards cooling their heels in there. Point is, it doesn't matter. You either have the money for a lawyer like me, or you don't. So your guy's getting off scot-free. In spite of his previous convictions, parole violations, you name it. It'll take a month, more or less, and he'll be back delivering flowers stuffed with cocaine." At that moment a package with another five thousand dollars landed with a thud on his desk. I could hear him opening it, picking up the receiver.

"Is that what I think it is, on your desk?" I asked him.

"Mr. X?" he answered. "It'll be one week, two at the most. Do we have a deal?"

"I'd shake on it," I growled, "but it's probably better if we kept our relationship distant. Oh, and one more thing. When this young man's fiancée comes to thank you, please do not reveal my existence. Simply say that you're taking the case on because it's so clearly a travesty of justice."

I said that you'd be proud of me, Roxanna. And it's a more profound therapy than the one I practiced with you. Instead of ordering some nonexistent scout to discover Simon, I've been training the kid myself, bought him a couple of basketball magazines, have been taking walks with him around the neighborhood. At times by ourselves, at times with Rose. I arrive early on nights when I'm asked to dinner and help Marta with the meal, get her lazy husband to chop onions. "Only you could have made me do it, Gus," Santos said. "Look at us," he added a few hours later, "the lot of us, all the men, washing the dishes, drying them, putting them away. You're going to make us into wimps, Gus. But for you, *mi amigazo*…"

I've even calmed them down, stopped them from quarreling boisterously all day long. For Rose's sake. Because you know what I discovered? That capacity of yours to pray while everybody around you was raising a ruckus. Roxanna, that was bull. But it accomplished its goal: to make me, back then, admire you even more. Rose, on the other hand, needs real quiet. That relentless sound has even made her, once in a while, skip the ceremony, not pray at all. You would never have done that, Roxanna, because you weren't praying for a real patient to get well. You were praying that I would believe you. Right? Did you get a bonus each time I fell for your trick? Do you get paid extra if the guy tries to bribe his guards and reach you? Do you use the prayer stratagem in each session? Or was it only for me?

So many things I'd like to ask you.

But I never will. Maybe I don't even need to find you anymore. As long as you do me this last service, Roxanna who was mine in my imagination and was really never mine: Listen to my plans, how I will cure myself forever of the demons I had before you came into my life, how I will cure myself of the other demons that came into my life when you left it.

I am going to help Rose escape from this existence she is trapped in, survive whether the factory goes under or doesn't.

You gave me the idea. Who made that up, you or Tolgate or some hack scriptwriter? That you wanted to go back to your native island, an exotic touch probably meant to enthrall me even further. What's clear is that this particular tropical dream most definitely did not stem from Rose. Though now she's considering it, now that I've brought it up.

We biked down to the river on Saturday, had a picnic, a lovely long intimate afternoon, just the two of us. Like a brother and a sister telling each other their secret lives. She mused about her own life, how she'd been born, things she had never revealed to anybody and me—I couldn't really confess who I was, where I came from, but did let her know, let it slip into the conversation, that for years I had thought my mother had taken her life, I came as close to confiding in her as I ever have to anyone else. And at some point, as the sun was setting on the riverbank, I planted the idea of a business future in her head, got her fantasizing about that possibility.

"I had a friend, you know," she said hesitantly, "from Puerto Rico— and she had that project, she would have been the perfect person for that sort of plan."

When I asked her what had happened to her friend, maybe we could include her in the project, Rose just shook her head. She's not around anymore, was all she would say.

"We'll do it for her, then," I said, "make her dream come true through you."

Though I played down the likelihood that the person I knew might really be interested. It was a chance in a thousand, I said, nothing to get our hopes up about. And didn't mention it again during the rest of the afternoon or at dinner that night, or Sunday either. Let it simmer in her mind, watched her later on the screen discussing it with her mother first, then with her father, her brothers, her friend Georgia. Watched her through my monitor embroider the idea, watched how they made fun of her in a gentle, teasing sort of way.

Today's the day, though. Monday. Start of the week, start of a new life.

Tonight I'll tell her that I've spoken with a contact at the Clean Earth headquarters and that they've been thinking about opening a new line of products: Roxanna's Dream Herbs. I'm naming them for you, Roxanna, not only because you inspired them. The truth is that that label will sell more than ordinary Rose any day. Over drinks at the Sad Dogs I'll tell my Rose. Not quite ready to reveal who I am yet. I'll have her fly to Houston to see the boss himself, the big guy, Graham Blake. And the doors will swing open, just like in the movies, just like in the romance novels you loved to read, maybe only pretended to read, Roxanna, and there I'll be, my back to the door. I'll turn around and show my face and not only my face: the product designed, the campaign ready, the contract drawn up, the tickets back to Bogotá for her and for Johnny if he wants to come along and for the rest of the family as well. And her eyes will light up like your eyes once did.

Tonight's the night.

But now. But now. Now. Now you come in to your apartment, not you, Roxanna, but Rose. She comes in to the room at noon. She's not supposed to be back at midday, not supposed to return until this afternoon, when I will pick her up outside the factory, the camera is supposed to capture us both later coming into this room.

Something's wrong. Something is terribly wrong.

She closes the door with a slam, Roxanna, she almost falls rushing through the doorway, slams the door shut as if it were a rat trap clamping on her, screams Sonofabitch, you fucking sonafobitch. Rose who never swears, never hurries, never—She slumps down against the door, crashes into the floor sobbing. She's been crying, Roxanna. Tears are streaming down her face, crumpling, staining the white nurse's dress— she's never worn her nurse-uniform outside work before. And there on the floor, crouched like a fetus, she begins to rock herself back and forth, singing in Spanish, a lullaby, the one you used to sing as well, Roxanna, that you learned from her, stole from Rose: she's singing it to herself, trying to put herself to sleep, trying to console herself for something or somebody or…

I can't figure out what's happening, what to do. If Sonia were here I—if this were a mock crisis, it would be so easy, a matter of pressing a button, ordering a close up, getting a computer reading and print out, asking Ivan to investigate, but now there's nothing I can do, just watch, pressed to my monitor.

Outside, Mrs. O'Leary is knocking on the door and I ignore her. "It's urgent, Mr. Henderson," she says, "Mrs. Owen's on the phone, Jessica Owen from Houston. She needs to talk to you." Jessica! She's tracked me down. The hell with her. The hell with the company. I sidle up to the door, keeping my eye on Rose, that bundle of sorrow and rocking despair that is my Rose. I call out, "I don't know any Mrs. Owen, Jessica or otherwise. That lady must have the wrong person, Mrs. O'Leary." I can hear old lady O'Leary trundling down the stairs, complaining about her arthritis, off to give Jessica a piece of her mind.

Now Rose is crawling on all fours, crawling across the living room that I have crossed myself so many times, where I played cards with Eduardo and Simon and Santos and that old fool José and watched late-night wrestling on TV, where Marta and Rose tried to teach me old Colombian songs, I once crossed a living room very much like the one I'm seeing now, crossed it to save you, Roxanna, thought I was saving you, thought you were dying. And I know where she's going, I know it as if I had scripted it myself: She's going to the bathroom, yes, she can barely stand up, but she's—

I use my cellular phone. Use it for the first time since I've been here. It's been turned off. Every time Jessica has tried me, every time Sam Halneck has tried and the office and my secretary and Hector and Dr. Tolgate and even the children, every call has been answered by a flat mechanical voice stating that I am out of reach, not even an answering machine to leave a message. I dial the lawyer who's taking care of Johnny's case. It takes less than a minute, but by then Rose has reached the bathroom, she's closed the bathroom door behind her, I switch to the camera that's positioned in there and Rose has hoisted herself up onto the toilet seat, slaps herself twice in despair, her face red as if she were being dried up, chewed up by her own hands. She rises, makes a lunge for the medicine cabinet, loses her balance, falls back onto her seat.

The lawyer says hello.

"What's happened to Johnny?" I ask.

"Nothing's happened to him," comes the reply. "He'll be out this week, like I—"

"Don't lie to me. They killed him. I know they killed him. Don't try to cover it up."

"Hey, easy, easy, take it easy. I just left Johnny, not less than an hour ago. He was in pretty good shape. Playing cards with the warden. Getting ready for his freedom. Something about turning a new leaf, starting off fresh with his girlfriend in Colombia. So if you know something that I don't know, I'm all ears. But if you're just blowing words through your ass—"

I hang up on him.

Johnny's alright. Rose is the one who's going to die. She's lifted herself to the sink, clawed at the medicine, now she's found the pills, she's gulping them down by the dozen. By the dozen.

I dial 911, tell them where to go, the suicide's name. I give them my real name, Blake, Graham Blake, hope they'll recognize it, hope that will hurry them up. Maybe I should have told them that my dad used to play golf at the Merion, maybe I should have—

I rush out the door and find Mrs. O'Leary mounting the stairs with her heavy fat legs.

"Mrs. Owen insists," she grunts. "She says it's an emergency. She says you'd better talk to her. Says your real name's not Henderson."

"I'll be back," I call out, as I bound down the stairs, bang my way out the door. I jump into my car and speed toward Rose's apartment. It's easier when everything is coordinated ahead of time, Roxanna. Right? When you have Sonia making believe she's conspiring, you have that other guy, his name was—what? Benjy?—you have him clearing the way, pretending he's kissing her, maybe taking advantage of the situation to really give her a good fondle because she can't complain, she can't move, Sonia couldn't give away the game. But they're not here now. No Tolgate to make sure I get to save you in time, Roxanna. No counterfeit pills down an illusive throat. Real pills, real throat, real vomit, real brain going into real convulsions. Real traffic jam. I won't ever make it to where she is, Roxanna, where you were waiting for me.

Using my cellular, I track down the ambulance that is already parked outside Rose's apartment building. They've found the woman! They're bringing her down!

I abandon the car in the middle of the traffic, just leave it there. I can run these last two blocks. Hold on, Rose. I'm on my way.

And reach her, just as the men are carrying her out on a stretcher. "Who are you?"

"Her husband," I lie. I grab her hand, hold on to its cold dead fingers, but she's alive, Roxanna, I've saved her again, for the second time, for the second time. I can feel life sifting back into her pulse, a slight tinge of pink in her cheeks, I sing the lullaby to her, the one with the Spanish words, hum them to her, make up the words, holding her head up so she won't gag, murmuring to her that it will be alright, it will be fine, everything's going to be alright.

I wait by her side in the hospital corridor, get her checked into the most exclusive suite, plunk my credit card down, superplatinum, spare no expense.

I let her sleep. I've given orders that no one else is to disturb us. I don't want the rest of the family scrambling in. Not before I understand what's happened. If it's not Johnny…

"I'm sorry, Gus," she says, suddenly, in a soft voice, calls me from across the room. I've been standing by the window, watching, watching. Not spying on anybody but the birds, not registering anything other than the wind going through the trees, counting the leaves as they fall, the patients down in the afternoon sun strolling, getting better. That's what I've been doing. Maybe praying, maybe that too.

"I am, really. Really, really sorry. I should have told you." She coughs, I try to stop her from speaking, but she wants to, she feels that she owes me an explanation. When I'm the one who owes her, who needs to explain things. That will come, that's coming. No need to hurry it up. She's back, I'm back, at the old pace, the simple gait of time taking its time. "I've done this before."

"What do you mean?"

"I should have told you. I'm sorry. I—I've tried to kill myself. More than once. Something just comes over me and I can't stand it anymore, I can't keep up a cheerful face, if I have to smile one more time I'll scream and that's what I do. I scream. But nobody hears me but me. And then I scream again and not even I hear myself scream and then something, somebody inside tells me what to do."

"But what happened? Yesterday you were so full of plans, I told you that today I'd have a surprise for you…"

"They never come true, my dreams," Rose says, and I believe her. The way she says it, I can't help but believe her.

"So today… ?"

"I lost my job. So did my papá."

"You lost your job? It can't be true."

She smiles, but it is not like any smile I've ever seen on her face or on yours, Roxanna. It's the smile of the defeated, the smile of those who are about to die and know it and can do nothing about it and don't want to give the enemy the satisfaction of seeing them recognize defeat. A smile without hope, without energy, without Roxanna.

"That's it. Before we could even go out on strike. We lost. Not one of us has a job now. Not one member in my family. And I—I just gave up. Like—like her."

"Her?"

"A friend of mine. What does it matter anyway? I'm sorry. God, I'm sorry. But at times it's just too much."

I'm the one who's smiling now, *laughing* would be a better word. She looks at me in astonishment. How can I be laughing at her disaster?

"What if I were to say"—I stutter the words through my laughter—"what if I were to tell you that I can have you reinstated like this." And I snap my fingers as if I were a magician.

"I'd say you're trying to cheer me up. But it's okay. You don't need to. I won't try to kill myself again. Because of this, I mean. I can't promise about other things, tomorrow, day after tomorrow. But I'm over this. Got it out of my system."

She's back to her old patient trudging ways, as slow, as patient, as ever. Except that now I know that underneath that surface there sleeps someone else, another Rose Montero who can monstruously rise up out of her deepest waters and destroy her. Unless that person inside is put to rest, kept at bay.

"You don't think I can get you your job back?"

"I'm not in the mood for jokes, Gus. You saved me and I'm grateful and all that, but—"

"What if I can swing it? What then?"

"I'm too tired to play games. Or argue. Swing it, Gus. Be my guest. *Adelante.*"

I pull out my cellular phone. I pull out my electronic directory. I look at her, to gauge her reaction. There is none. She's staring up at the empty ceiling.

I call the manager of the factory. He's in a meeting.

"Well, tell him to get his butt out of there."

Still no reaction from Rose. She must think I'm making believe, calling the delicatessen or my mother or some friend who's in on the joke. She still thinks I'm trying to cheer her up.

"Who shall I say is calling?" The secretary on the other end of the line is icy.

"Tell him Graham Blake."

I watch to see what Rose thinks. Rose manages a wan smile. This is cheering her up. I'm pretending I'm the biggest boss of them all. She didn't think I had the nerve.

Rose can't hear what the secretary is saying on the other end. "Mr. Blake, we've been looking for you for the last week and a half. Your wife's been—This is Mr. Blake, right?"

"Look, do I sound like the Easter Bunny? Get your boss on the line. Now."

Rose's grin grows wider. I wink at her. She manages to wink back.

There is a pause, then Paul St. Martin comes on.

"Paul?"

"Graham, my God, where have you been? Your kids are... Jessica's been worried sick. I think she tracked you down today. Are you really in Philadelphia?"

"I'm definitely here in Philadelphia. Now you tell me. What in the hell's happening at my factory? I've been informed that you got rid of two employees today. Santos Montero. Rose Montero."

"Not just those two. We're giving the pink slips to a third of the personnel. Before they can call a strike. Non-essentials first. By next week the rest will be gone. We're closing down the plant."

"What do you mean, closing down the plant?"

"Moving it to Thailand, it seems. Jessica's been trying to get you. Talk to her."

"I don't want to talk to her. I want Rose Montero put back on the job. Is that understood? And her father, Santos. Santos as well. In fact I want him promoted to head of security."

"I'm afraid I can't do that, Graham. I'm taking orders directly from Jessica and the board of directors. They told me you might call and that I was to route any complaints back to them."

"I want you to listen and I want you to listen carefully. I'm going to be at the factory tomorrow, and you'd better have that door wide open, because I'm coming in and I'm talking to all the workers, including the Monteros, Rose and Santos. Have everybody meet me in the cafeteria—at seven-thirty in the morning. We'll get both shifts then."

I hang up on Paul.

Rose is sitting up in bed. My conversation has energized her. "That's the way to tell them, Gus. You are the most incredible man. What a trickster! What sheer—what's the word—chutzpah!"

I try to concentrate on her adorable Latino accent saying that Jewish word. I try not to think about what I'm about to do.... Then I plunge in, Roxanna. Just as I did with you. The truth. It's not the way I expected to reveal my identity, but here goes:

"I'm not Gus. Gus Henderson's not really my name."

There's an edge to my voice, a steeliness that signals to her that I'm not joking, this is not a new level of banter and fantasy.

"I'm Graham Blake. The chief executive officer of Clean Earth. I own your factory, Rose."

She still doesn't believe me. But she's getting there. She needs just one little push to be convinced.

I grab the phone again and dial Houston headquarters, the ultra-private number, the one only I know.

Jessica answers.

"Jessica? This is Graham."

"Graham! I've been—"

"How dare you close down the factory here in Philadelphia without my approval."

"It's that or lose the Company, Graham. The Board is ready to dump you. Your latest conduct has persuaded them that you're... you're unreliable. Granger's made a hostile bid and he may have the votes, unless we—How dare you simply walk out on us during the two most crucial weeks we've ever been through?"

"Well, I'm back now. And you're not closing down anything, here or anywhere else. Understood?"

"Graham, if you'd answered your phone—"

"Clean Earth is not closing my dad's factory down. Tell Granger to go fuck himself. I'll see you tomorrow in Philadelphia. Tomorrow at seven-thirty. In the cafeteria."

And I hang up on her as well.

I turn to Rose. She is looking at me in a way I have never seen before—and it is not the look of admiration that I saw on your face, Roxanna, not the look of desire I had hoped for on yours or hers. It is—how to describe it, Roxanna, you who have tried on all the faces, rehearsed so many alternatives in your multiple roles. Except perhaps this one. Tolgate must have forbidden you this one. You'd never be allowed to wear a face of such unadulterated, pure hatred. That's what Rose is feeling toward her savior: a rancor that threatens to twist her face beyond recognition.

I don't think she hears me, she's not even listening, I think.

I explain everything anyway. All of it. From the start. I explain my insomnia, my headaches, my wish to create a better world, all the wonderful inventions of Clean Earth, the crisis. I explain you to her, Rox-anna, the Corporate Life Therapy Institute in Houston, the clinic here in Philadelphia, everything, how I screwed you over, Roxanna, and then rescued you. How I was cured and how something worse began to take over my life. How I discovered her. What I did, what I've been doing. How I spied on her. How I saved her. How I'm going to save Johnny.

She still says nothing.

"You're going to get your job back, Rose," I say. "Not that you really need it. I intend to set up a new division at Clean Earth." I tell her about Roxanna's Dream Herbs, my plans for her to return to Colom-bia, open up the Latino market.

She finally breaks her silence. With one word.

"Why?"

Why? Why, Roxanna? Why am I doing this, did this? What can I answer? Not the truth: not that I insanely need her to tell me I am good, that the smile in her mouth and the fire in her eyes and the words on her tongue should all cradle me like a child lost and then found again. I can't. I can't tell her that, because then I could never be sure that if it comes, it would be spontaneous and true. So I let go with an enigmatically obscure phrase: "That's something you're going to have to figure out for yourself."

She rolls out of the bed with alacrity, almost as if she weren't ill, hadn't been knocked out by twenty pills less than four hours ago.

And she insults me, Roxanna. Insults me as you would have insult-ed me, would have kicked me, if you had been a real woman and not a paid performer eager to get a good bonus from Tolgate once I declared my satisfaction. I don't want to repeat what she said, the words you never said to me. She told me to get the fuck out of that room and the fuck out of her life and the fuck off this planet. She said I was off my rocker, a pervert, a voyeur, a heartless monster. She said my greed had almost destroyed her family, had caused her more pain than I could ever imagine. I was the shadow figure who had been behind years of bad luck, I was the one who had driven her to suicide so many times, taken her best friend away from her, the face that would haunt her forever. "I'd have to wash for twenty years, soak for twenty years, submerge myself in water for twenty years, rub myself for a million years, and I still wouldn't be rid of your stench, the smell of your lies. It clings to me, fills me, fills me. And the worst thing is you think you're Mother Teresa. You think I need a Mother Teresa?"

I let her pour scorn on me. Let her slap my face. Let her spit on me. I let her spend her spite on me.

She was acting her rage out and yours as well. I could feel you egging her on from somewhere, Roxanna, the performance you would have loved to give. If you hadn't been handed a script full of redemption and softy-feely goody-goodiness.

I kept my calm because I craved that punishment, I liked it, I deserved it. It was cleansing me, her maternal rage, making me pure again. I kept my calm because I knew that I would have the last say, I knew that tomorrow I would be the one in charge. Tomorrow I would prove her wrong about who I was.

When she tumbled back on the bed, breathless, still angry, without energy and still without having extracted even one word from me in my own defense, that's when I said to her:

"You owe me one favor. For saving your life. One favor. Will you do that for me?"

"Get out!"

"I want you to come tomorrow to the meeting with the workers at the factory. You and your father. And bring your whole family along. Can you do that?"

She didn't answer, but I knew she'd be there, I knew she would come to hear me in that cafeteria where I had first seen her through the lens of a camera, where I had myself discovered as a child the ways in which my charms made me invulnerable and invincible.

I slept well during the night. Surprised myself. Awakening only once just before dawn, gently coming out of my dreams to find the question there, staring me in the face stark and naked, almost like the body of a woman next to me in the darkness. Was Tolgate behind all of this? That question.

Tolgate must have been hatching a plan, preparing a scenario for my therapy well before I had come to see him, probably before Sam Halneck had even mentioned the Corporate Life Therapy Institute to me, maybe even before I was aware that a crisis was looming, Tolgate must have been waiting for a long time for Graham Blake, CEO, to cross his threshold, one of a long list of potential patients he kept his eyes on. He could not have organized all that infrastructure, those actors at their perfect pitch, that carefully designed apartment, without a protracted pre-production schedule. The research alone must have taken him months. Had he decided, early on, that a suicide, your fake suicide, Roxanna, would transform and climax our relationship? Marshaled everything, pushed this button and that button, so that I wound up watching you in that bathroom, so that I would inevitably try to rescue you? Did he probe my family history, come upon my mother's illness, decide that to have another woman die in front of my eyes was the one sure way to jolt me into action? And did he rummage about for a woman to model you on, Roxanna, seek someone who had, in her own life, a history of attempted suicide? Someone who, when I searched her out as I eventually must, would repeat your gesture, Roxanna? Would try to take her life, orchestrating me to reveal myself to her and crazily promise her I would keep the factory even if it meant losing Clean Earth?

And inside the spiral of my thoughts inside thoughts, Roxanna, this one at the very bottom of the mud of my swirling identity: Had he chosen Rose because she was suicidal, had my doctor conveniently discovered how sick she was when he stumbled upon her existence, or had he, on the contrary, fabricated her, had his eye on her as he had kept his eye on me for many years, cornered her slowly with a series of actions and manipulations that had led her to the sort of despair I had witnessed yesterday? Had he cut his costs, used her and her family in other corporate treatments, used her to cure people like Hank Granger, Sam

Halneck, who knows how many others? Worked on her, scripted her, the way he had worked on me? Was it that invisible shadow of Tolgate that had driven her in the past to try to take her own life?

There was no way of ever knowing the answer to these questions.

There was only my decision, tomorrow, which would make them irrelevant, which would set Rose free, put her finally beyond the grasp of people like Tolgate. Beyond the grasp of people like Graham Blake.

Tomorrow is today, Roxanna. It is now.

Now that I stand in front of a packed auditorium at seven-thirty in the morning. At the very back of the cafeteria is Rose. She has on her blue dress, your blue dress, Natasha's. Fitting that she's wearing it now, on the last day of this adventure.

Lurking in a corner unobtrusively is Paul St. Martin, pale and drawn. When he greeted me at the gate, he handed me a message from Jessica: "Board meeting this afternoon at four P.M. in Houston to make final decision. Be there." I crumpled it, felt like throwing it in the air and swatting it like a tennis ball into the nearest trash can, but inserted it in my pocket instead. I can feel it now, scratching at my thigh through the lining, reminding me that after I speak here, I will have to board a plane and speak somewhere else, have to sustain what I am about to promise here.

What I say is really quite simple. I'm not good at speeches.

I explain to the assembly of workers that the decision to close the factory was made behind my back, the board taking advantage of the fact that I have been away. Where I have been, in fact, is among them. I have gone back to the age-old way in which men in power discover how to redress injustice: by disguising themselves and living among the people whose fate they must determine. So that my decision should be reached not as if it affected others, faraway others, images on a screen, but as if it affected my own life. As if I were the one to be thrown out of a job without training for a new one. As if I were the one who would come home to tell my wife that we have to skimp on the sugar. As if I were the one who had to walk to the park with my eldest daughter and let her know she can't go to college. As if I were the one who watches the woman I love try to kill herself because she can't take it anymore.

I tell them I'm going back to Houston and I'm going to defend this factory. I'm going to keep it open, just as my father would have expected me to. As my mother would have wanted me to. No moving it to Mexico or Thailand, Turkey or Brazil. Here in the U.S. And if that means that I lose everything else, well, I'll come back here to work with them. Even if this is the only factory left to me. I'll start from zero. We'll lick this thing together.

They are silent at the end. In a way the best reaction, the best homage. Not the easy applause. Each one comes up afterward, thanks me, shakes my hand. Including my family. One by one. They understand why I infiltrated their lives. So I could defend those very lives. They still love me, approve of what I'm doing.

Rose is the last one.

I had kept my eye on her during the whole speech, watched her gaze changing, foretold that a smile would dawn as it did, cajoled out of her with my words the admiration I need. The look you gave me, Roxanna: I wanted that look again, one more time, telling me I am a wonderful man, a good man. Telling me that I can sleep at night because I am doing what I believe is right, no matter what the consequences.

Rose and not Roxanna saying this to me. The real woman, not the actress. My script and not his, not Tolgate's. My life.

We walk out together to my car.

"I've been thinking about your offer," she says. The first thing she said since she demanded that I get the hell out of her hospital room yesterday afternoon. "I've decided to reject it, going back to Colombia and all that."

I wait.

"You can't just save me, Gus," she said. "Just my family. I couldn't. Leave all of them behind, these people. Cure them every day, pray for them every night, and then one morning just up and leave because you happened to take a fancy to me. I couldn't."

"Even if it means not living out your dreams?"

"I am living out my dreams," she says.

"And your nightmares."

"And my nightmares," she agrees. "That's the way it is. This is my country now."

I get in the car. "Roxanna's Dream Herbs. You don't want to miss out on that, have somebody else in charge. I'll be waiting for you."

"You can't just save me, Gus," she says, and gives me that look for one last final time, that look I need to get me on my way, that look I keep warm and clean inside me as I drive off to the most important meeting of my life.

You would be proud of me, Roxanna.

NINE

" **I** 've never told anybody this," she
says. "Can I trust you?"

"Yes."

"Can I really trust you,
Gus?" she says.

"I'm good at keeping
secrets."

"I want to tell you," she says,
"in fact I've been waiting for somebody that I can... Somebody... "

"Anybody?"

"Not anybody, Gus," she says. "Somebody
I can trust, I've been hoping to be able to find
someone to tell this to."

"How about Johnny? He'll be free in a few days, if
what you say is true, he'll—"

"Not Johnny," she says. "You."

"We've got all afternoon."

"I have to get back. Dinner," she says. "Saturday dinners are sacred. I promised my mamá…"

"I'm sure she'll understand."

"She will," she says. "They all will, my brothers, my father… What do you think of my father?"

"I like him. Santos is a good man."

"He is a good man," she says. "What I have to tell you concerns him. What nobody here knows."

"Nobody knows? How can you be sure?"

"I love this riverbank," she says. "I love the water and the trees and the sunlight and all those people taking their time. Life like the Delaware flowing by."

"And the flowers."

"The flowers, yes," she said. "Do you remember that I told you that my father hadn't been by my mother's side for my birth? Do you remember that?"

"Yes. You said he'd seen you for the first time when you came to the States. Not even a photo, you said."

"For years," she says, "the only thing I knew was that he had got into some sort of trouble that night of my birth—and the less I knew about that, the better, I thought. I thought it might have something to do with—you know, drugs."

"Drugs? I don't think so. Not your dad."

"That's just what I thought," she says. "I could never imagine him mixed up in anything like that, just like Johnny, I mean—But just in case, I never asked, I never wanted to know. Except… "

"Except… ?"

"There have been… inquiries," she says. "Questions. Two men—policemen, they said they were—they came around. First when Evangelina—a friend you never met, she—anyway, they came around and now, lately, again, asking about my father. Insistently."

"That's harassment. You should—"

"Gus, Gus," she says. "What world do you live in, *Dios mío*? You don't file charges against cops—or whoever they were—just because they come to ask questions. Who'd listen to me? Or even believe me? And they seemed harmless enough. And… and I didn't have anything to tell them anyway."

"You really didn't know anything?"

"Only a bit," she says. "My father had come to Catalina in the early sixties to install the one telephone line and then stayed on as its lone operator. Nobody knew where he came from, the mysterious Santos Montero, or where he was going afterward, except that he was studying English by correspondence and that he said he would one day emigrate to the United States where he had a *compadre* waiting for him, he was always putting on airs about how he wasn't going to stay there forever. People admired him, believed everything he told them: *después de todo*, he had brought the phone to Catalina, he could speak two languages!"

"He was their link to the outside world."

"Right," she says. "And of course he was a charmer, he still is, can get you to bark at the moon if he feels like it. He mesmerized the whole town. Well, almost. Not the Aguirres, my mother's family. They didn't trust him. Or anybody from the outside world. And my father's reaction to that mistrust was typical: He decided—very deliberately, according to my mother—to seduce her, Marta, the youngest Aguirre girl, who was only fifteen at the time, just to show her father and brothers that he could do it."

"And he did it with flowers."

"Yes, Gus," she says. "Words and flowers. He started to explore the *comarca* and search out a different sort of flower each morning, never repeating himself and he'd send her the flower, each one with a poem. Maroon flowers with a gold tail and white snowbird flowers and fuchsia trumpet all pink and pristine white flowers with long stems and erect spikes and the infract species where the newest buds emerge from where the last flower shriveled and fell off and the cool wonder of the

masdevallia blue hanging upside-down so blue so blue and the pepper-
mint flowers that grow all year long and the handlebar mustache that
grows on certain single flowers and—I know all about this because I've
read those poems, I've read how he made something up for each one
like a perfume of words, how he grew a mustache only to go with the
flower, how he found an orchid that smelled like red coconut cream pie,
how he went crazy for her, for little Marta. It took him a year, but there
was no stopping him, and there it was, my mother ended up with my
brother Eduardo in her belly."

"So what did the family say, how did they react?"

"My mother told her family," she says, "about the affair and the
same day my father came to the house dressed in his only good suit and
offered to marry her, but her father and brothers, instead of opening a
bottle of rum and celebrating, well, they beat him up, threw him out,
threatened to kill him."

"So that's why your father left?"

"Not at all,"`she says. "In typical Santos Montero fashion he mar-
ried her anyway—two weeks later snuck her out of the house and had
the priest perform the ceremony. According to my mother because my
father knew things about the priest from phone calls that had come in
or gone out, I wouldn't put it past my papá to eavesdrop a bit and use
the information."

"And your mother?"

"She adored him," she says, "and believed that the Aguirres would
come around when the baby was born, but in fact it got worse, they
wouldn't speak to her, they made life impossible for both of them, so
much so that my mother decided that they had to leave Catalina and
start all over again somewhere else. My father agreed, they'd move to
the States as soon as he saved enough money. But that wasn't the real
reason, according to my mother. The real reason was that nobody was
going to run Santos Montero out of town, this town or any town.
Except that they did—they finally ran him out of town the night I was

born. And that's where the story stopped. My mother never wanted to tell me the rest of it and my brother didn't know it and as we'd been cut off from grandparents and relatives and friends from back then, there was nobody to tell me. And that was alright with me. Alright until those men came by and got me thinking again."

"So you asked him."

"What I'm going to tell you now…" she says. "If anybody finds out…"

"You don't have to tell me. You can stop right now."

"It was the fault of that man Onassis," she says.

"Onassis? The Greek tycoon?"

"I asked my father," she says, "waited for him at the Sad Dogs one night, slipped into his booth, asked him. It took a while, he downed a couple of whiskeys, said this and that and then: 'October twentieth, 1968,' he said, nice and calm. 'Does that date say anything to you?' 'The day I was born,' I said. 'The day Jackie Kennedy was married to Onassis,' my papá said. 'He bought Jackie a ring worth one and a quarter million dollars—ruby and diamonds. Onassis bought that ring,' my father said, 'and then he picked up the phone and called me. It was October seventeenth, 1968, and you were born three days later.' What's the matter, Gus?"

"I'm—I'm just surprised, I guess. I didn't expect this sort of story, this—"

"Yes," she says, "millionaires make me nervous too."

"No. It's not that. I don't understand what Onassis has to do with—?"

"Onassis had been told," she says, "that in a little village in Colombia called Catalina people grew the best and freshest orchids in the world. Orchids at that time of the year. Enough to fill the yacht *Christina* and the I-don't-know-what island, enough to make the guests in the chapel and the photographers faint with pleasure, those orchids, enough to make Jackie Kennedy realize what real love was, what real money can buy. According to my father, Onassis said, 'I want to buy all the orchids you have, every last one. For my marriage,' Onassis said, 'to the most glamorous woman in the world.' And my father was lucky or unlucky enough to be the lone phone operator and to have been studying English for the last seven years in order to escape Colombia and make it big up North. And right then and there he agreed on a price with Onassis, ten times the regular price..."

"Your father took a cut of the deal?"

"Ten percent commission," she says. "Enough to get us out of there. And he told Onassis that the flowers would be waiting for the plane and gave him instructions on where it should land and they agreed on the date, October nineteenth in the morning, and everything else. And my father had then gone and told everyone in town about the deal and had decided to let bygones be bygones and sent the priest to the Aguirres to include them in the deal and, *qué me dices*, there was a family reconciliation. For years they hadn't spoken to him, and now suddenly Onassis and his money changed all that."

"Greed. If he'd had lots of cash when he first arrived in Catalina, they would have accepted your father with open arms."

"Greed," she says, "yes."

"But how come the Aguirres and everybody else in town believed him?"

"Because he knew English," she says, "and he was the one with the phone, with the power, the connection to the world of the *gringos*, the man who would make them filthy rich. So they cut down every orchid in town and they carted them off to the field that served as an airstrip in the middle of the hills, and the mayor had my papá translate his speech into English to deliver to the men who would come for the orchids, even if nobody expected Onassis himself to come or even any member of his family, but still, the children were going to sing the national anthem and *Flores a María*, and the same priest who married my parents was going to bless the flowers and..."

"And what?"

"And they waited and they waited, Gus," she says. "All the dawn of the nineteenth and during the day and all the night, and the morning of the twentieth, more than twenty-four hours went by and they just stood there, only one or another of them leaving from time to time to bring food and drink, as if they thought that if they fell asleep, the plane wouldn't come, and then they heard a sound on the horizon, over the hills and beyond the trees and a plane, a plane they all cried out, except that it was thunder, it was a storm coming. It poured on them, on the whole town, all of them still waiting for the Onassis plane, for fortune to fall on them from the sky and only rain came. And then someone, who had gone back for an umbrella, a woman, maybe one of my Aguirre aunts, returned and said that on the radio it had been announced that Jackie and Onassis had already been married, at five fifteen P.M. on some Greek island…"

"Skorpios."

"And that it had been raining there too," she says, "a cold, bleak rain, not like our warm storms in Colombia, but what mattered was that the marriage had already happened and that there had been no orchids from Colombia or anywhere else at the wedding. All sorts of other flowers, but no orchids. And by then they started, the people from the town, but especially my mother's family, they started to look for my father. Where's Santos Montero? Where did that conniving *hijo de puta* go?"

"And where had he gone?"

"He was back home," she says, "where my mother was having spasms and pangs and her *dolores*, and as the crowd began to gather outside and their bad mood turned ever more sour and angry, my papá decided to slip out the back door. He gave mamá a fleeting kiss on the forehead and asked her to call me Jacqueline if I was a girl but not Aristoteles if I was a boy, to show that he bore no grudges to the bride— always a gentleman, my papá. You'll send for us?, mamá asked. And he said, I won't touch a drop of alcohol until I see this baby again, I swear it on my mother's grave. And he kept his promise: He saved every last penny, not even a drink, so that he could see me. He promised that and—"

"Quite a promise."

"For my father, yes," she says, "he made that promise and then he headed for the escape hatch. He'd built the house himself, with no help from anybody, made sure there was a back way out, so even then he must have thought he'd need it someday. And… "

"And… ?"

"That's the story," she says.

"That's it? The secret?"

"That's it," she says. "What do you think?"

"What do you mean?"

"Well," she says, "can I believe my father? For starters, did Onassis make that call? I mean, I've never been able to ask anybody, just myself."

"I don't understand."

"Maybe my father invented that call," she says, "had been planning his revenge on the Aguirres all those years—that's what they thought, anyhow, according to my father. To ruin them, make fools of them. For revenge. Or maybe he was, you know, delusional, I think that's the word, *loco*, convinced himself Onassis had called, convinced himself that he could save the town from backwardness and be a hero to its inhabitants, really be accepted as one of them."

"Or maybe there really was a call, maybe Onassis really wanted those flowers."

"It's possible," she says. "And it was that millionaire who was playing around with my father, betrayed him."

"It doesn't seem, though, like such a secret, so hard to find out. All you have to do is ask your mother."

"I did, Gus," she says. ` "And she didn't want to speak about it, still doesn't. The very next day, as soon as I started to—my mother cut me off. I had never heard her so sure of something. Not one more word, she said. One more word will kill me. I don't want to hear what he says happened."

"Why not?"

"Maybe," she says, "it never happened the way my father says, maybe he made the whole thing up, Onassis and the orchids and everything else, and she doesn't want me to think he's a liar. Or maybe there's another truth, more painful than this one, some other secret, something only she and he know about. Something too—well, terrible for her to remember, for her to tell me. Or she doesn't want to relive the pain of losing her father and mother and—Whatever the reason, she's going to take that secret to her grave."

"And you don't want anybody asking her about it?"

"My mother's a very private person, Gus," she says.

"There's a way of finding out. There's a way, you know."

"Is there?" she says.

"Going back. Going back to Catalina and asking. You haven't returned to Colombia since you left, right? Maybe I can help you to—"

"I don't need to go back, Gus," she says. "I like the story just like it is now. If my papá made it up, I like to think that he made it up for me, so I could hear it someday when I was ready, what he'd wished he'd done to make me into a princess, to give me everything my heart desired. How he hoped he would strike it rich. And if it's true, well, it explains why I'm known as the *niña de las flores*, if you think that I was born with the smell of thousands of orchids wilting and dying in the rain waiting to be moved halfway across the world for somebody's wedding, those flowers greeting me as they died and staying with me even as they were thrown into the garbage and carted away, their smell and their friendship ever since, blessing me."

"So you're their daughter."

"Yes," she says. "The daughter of the flowers."

"The daughter of the flowers. And why are you telling this to me, of all people?"

"You've been," she says, "so good to us. This story is the one thing that belongs to me, only to me. The story of how I was made, why I am the way I am. It's my gift to you."

"Your gift to me."

"Yes," she says. "And because I know I can trust you with this story. I know I can trust you."

"Yes," Graham Blake says, "you can trust me."

EPILOGUE

"A man always has two reasons for what he does.
A good reason and the real reason."

—J. P. MORGAN

"Is it time to wake up?"

—PEDRO CALDERÓN DE LA BARCA
Life Is a Dream

TEN

You asked me to let you know what happened, Jessica. You wanted to know every last detail.

Following your suggestion, I met your husband—former husband, that is —at the airport. He was, of course, surprised to see me.

"Tolgate! What in hell are you doing here?" he asked. "Go and torment somebody else."

I told him this was no way to treat someone who had shepherded him to where he now was: about to encounter true illumination. Or did he think that all this was a coincidence, did he really think that this second trip of his to Philadelphia had not all along been anticipated, an essential part of the original therapy?

He had evidently considered that possibility on his own, but he couldn't help but be interested in the fact that I was admitting it so openly. And then, of course, he immediately did not like feeling interested, began to worry right away—he is a worrier, Jessica, of that there can be no doubt—worry that I was trying to snare him again, just as I had that first night of his treatment when the actress we called Roxanna walked into the room he was spying on.

I showed him my hands, both palms upward. "Empty," I said. "No tricks."

He smiled at that. Or smiled at something else. But nevertheless it was a smile. And then he pushed on, past me.

"Your wife asked me to come get you," I said to his back. Not because this would stop him. It did. But because it was true and I had no intention of playing dirty. All the cards were laid out on the table. Well, not every last one of them. I have had to keep certain information to myself. Keep it from all those involved, including you. Otherwise this treatment would never work.

"What wife?"

"Former wife," I corrected myself. "Jessica. She wanted me to drive you to Clean Earth headquarters. And give you a chance to talk to me before you make your decision."

"I've already made my decision."

I reminded him that he had expressed a similar conviction that first night when he had violently announced that he was leaving, that the treatment I was proposing was immoral, that he wanted no part of it.

"That's what I should have done," he said, and started again toward the exit, the taxi stand.

"You can't mean that," I answered, keeping up with his long strides. "Just because the ride was rough doesn't mean you repent of it. Would you ever be where you are today, with the stark choices that confront you today, if you hadn't been through all of this?"

"What stark choices?"

"I really believe, Mr. Blake, that you would do well to let me drive you into town. In the worst of cases, you'll have saved your taxi fare. Or maybe, in a better scenario, saved something more substantial."

He faltered, Jessica. He was afraid of me, you see. That's what he understood, standing there. Because he was afraid, he needed to come with me. He needed to go through this last test.

We walked in silence to the parking lot, got in my Lincoln, and neither of us uttered another word until we reached the freeway. He was the one to open fire.

"How come you know everything about me?"

"Nobody knows everything about anybody else. You don't even know everything about yourself."

"Not a good answer."

"Then ask a good question."

There was a calm in him, Jessica, an almost melodramatic calm. He believed in his calm, at least. He was sure of it.

"Since when have you been spying on me?"

"I don't think that really matters, Mr. Blake, and I wouldn't call it spying. You came to me, put yourself in my hands, asked me to provide therapy. I told you it was unorthodox."

"A mild word, Tolgate, *unorthodox*," he said. "Immoral. Illegal. Criminal. Murderous. Those are the words I would use. But you're not answering any of my questions."

"Let's see if you find one that I can answer."

"Are they all actors? Actresses?"

"Everybody in the world is acting out some sort of role, Mr. Blake. You are, I am, Roxanna was. The question is who writes our words: if we write them or somebody else does. Is there any doubt that this is the matter we really need to address: who is in control?"

"So Rose is also an actress? Is that what you're saying? Rose and her family?"

"Did she seem unreal to you?"

"She seemed all too real to me. Which is precisely why I'm asking you if she's an actress."

"If you don't know the answer to that," I said to him, slowing down as a large van full of nuns in front us put on the brakes, "I certainly can't furnish it. And you're in even more trouble than I could have foretold. Next question."

He paused and then said:

"Why?"

He said that one word and then something happened to his face, Jessica, as if he were remembering another occasion when he uttered that word or heard it in somebody else's mouth.

"Why did we organize the treatment this way? Because you needed it. Because you had to go through all this to face yourself, reach the final stage of your therapy, Mr. Blake. It has been awaiting you for the last six months, along with something you have put off time and again. Ever since the day when your crisis started, when you postponed this moment. It's time to end your insomnia."

"You mean time to wake up."

"Call it any way you want. You must now decide whether you hold on to your father's old Philadelphia plant and risk losing the rest of your Company, have it gobbled up by Mr. Granger, become a minor player in the business world, bankrupt, ruined. Or you can, on the other hand, sacrifice that plant and save your Company—"

"And become like Granger, a clone of Granger—"

"I would say make sure your company goes in the direction you want it to, continues saving lives and supplying healthy products, dream herbs, right? In either case you will have grown up. Isn't that what any therapy demands? Learn to live with yourself, the consequences of being yourself, even if you don't always like what that self is, really is?"

"And what do you think that self of mine should do?"

We had arrived in front of the giant glittering corporate headquarters of Clean Earth. I parked the car in the bus lane, ignoring the irate horns and claxons and curses.

"My opinion is irrelevant," I said. "These are the last minutes we will spend together. As soon as you descend from this car, I will cease to be your doctor. The therapy consists in bringing you this far. No more."

Your former husband opened the door on his side. Not stepping out yet.

"Who owns the Corporate Life Therapy Institute?" he asked.

"Investors who had faith that it would give them a good profit. Why? Are you interested in putting some capital into our little venture? You and I are both, after all, in the same business: making sure human beings stay healthy. Clean Earth could conceivably have a Clean Soul division. Why not?"

Graham gave a little laugh, Jessica. More like a bark. A bit bitter.

"I don't believe that our interests are compatible," he said. "Not to mention the scope of our operations. I deal with, affect, millions of people around the world. You deal with just a few."

"Yes," I answered, "but the few I deal with determine what happens to those millions."

He waited for me to say something else. I just looked at him, quietly, quietly. He swiveled his body, placed his feet out on the curb. Then turned back to me. It was strange to see his neck twisted like that, as if the head were about to come loose. Almost as if it belonged to somebody else. "One last question, Dr. Tolgate."

I let him take his time asking it.

"Do you sleep well at night, Dr. Tolgate?"

"As well as you will, Mr. Blake."

He looked at me and rose out of the car. He shut the door gently behind him, as if he did not want to hurt the metal, make too much noise.

His eyes went up, up, up to the office where you were waiting for him, Jessica, you and the board.

Then he crossed the plaza.

If you need one, I'll get you a copy of the video tape of our conversation. It ends, of course, with that moment when he reaches the building. When he disappears into the East Tower which houses the

Clean Earth Company. Like Jonah, if you will permit me for once to be biblical, being swallowed by the whale.

What he did next you already know.

ACKNOWLEDGMENTS

It goes without saying that only the company and fellowship, support and infinite patience, of those around me allowed *Blake's Therapy* to ever make its solitary way into the world. Let me name, therefore, the foremost culprits.

If this novel is dedicated, with thanks, to my eldest son, Rodrigo, who has so frequently collaborated with me on plays, scripts and films, it is because without his unflagging presence as I wrote there would have been no book. He not only helped me to imagine, from the very start, the different stages of Blake's trajectory and treatment but also constantly enlightened my own parallel quest with observations and guidance. Later on it was my wife Angélica's turn to come to my aid: As my first and best and most incisive reader, her frank advice and faultless critical faculties were, as usual, indispensable.

Dan Simon, my editor at Seven Stories, has proven to be an exceptional soulmate. He pushed me gently and respectfully to take another long and hard look at the manuscript, allowing me to deepen its humanity and explore the multiple implications of Blake's choices. Not to mention some of Dan's other penetrating editorial suggestions. I look forward to many years of working with him and his enthusiastic colleagues at the Press.

I owe an immense debt of gratitude to Tom Englehardt. He was my first editor in the English language when I started publishing at Pantheon almost twenty years ago and has since then remained steadfast in his friendship. His belief in my work and in this book in particular have been instrumental in its publication. In the cutthroat times that we live in, Tom's altruism is almost unbelievable and always inspiring.

Thanks as well to Jin Auh, who represents me at the Wylie Agency and who steered *Blake's Therapy* through its marathon course toward the light of day, invariably cheerful and encouraging. And then there is Hortensia Calvo, the Latin American Librarian at Duke University, who not only provided me with tons of material but also mentioned, very casually, as we searched for appropriate books and articles, a certain story about a town full of orchids in her native Colombia. And Raquel de la Concha in Madrid, my agent for the Spanish and Portuguese language, who suggested that I accept the offer by my Brazilian publisher, Roberto Feith, of *Objetiva*, that I write a short novel on this subject—which turned out to be the first incarnation of *Blake's Therapy*. And Margaret Lawless, then my assistant, who guarded my time with fierceness. And I could go on and on: Joaquín and Melissa and Isabella and…

But I should not end these notes of appreciation without thanking my hosts at the World Economic Forum who invited me to Davos a few years ago. I journeyed as a Fellow Forum to that town in Switzerland where the business and political leaders of the world gather each February. The real, the secret reason for my voyage there was the chance being afforded me to observe, at close range, the community to which my protagonist—who was already buzzing around in my head—supposedly